"Amy Mezulis is a brilliant psychologist and scientist who bri
this important and practical book to help teens help them
In plain, accessible language, Mezulis explains what depres
of actions—many of them low cost or no cost—that teens can take to work out of a
downward spiral of depression."

 —Janet S. Hyde, PhD, professor emeritus of psychology and gender and
  women's studies at the University of Wisconsin—Madison, and coauthor
  of *The Psychology of Women and Gender*

"Having witnessed the devastating impact of depression on adolescents in my personal life, I am thrilled to endorse this resource. Mezulis presents evidence-based,
psychoeducational information in a manner that is 'right-sized,' accessible, and engaging. She then integrates it into interactive exercises that will equip teens with tools
for recovery and coping. *Reversing the Spiral of Depression for Teens* is an invaluable
tool for teens, clinicians, and parents."

 —Lynette H. Bikos, PhD, ABPP, board certified in counseling psychology;
  professor and chair in the department of clinical psychology at Seattle
  Pacific University; and author of *ReCentering Psych Stats*

"*Reversing the Spiral of Depression for Teens* contains evidence-based, practical
tools for teens to use to help improve their mood and challenge their depression.
Mezulis offers easy-to-read and relatable materials to help teens understand their
depression and make change across several aspects of their lives—from sleep to exercise, motivation, and self-esteem. This self-help book is a great option for teens
who may face barriers to accessing other mental health treatment."

 —Jaclyn T. Aldrich, PhD, clinical assistant professor of pediatrics at the
  Ohio State University, and psychologist at Nationwide Children's Hospital

"Mezulis uses clear language to illustrate complex ideas in ways that are understandable to parents and teens. This book offers science-backed insights into what depression looks like, what can trigger it, and what can keep people trapped in it. Accessible language and engaging exercises help identify an individual's unique experience with depression, and offer strategies that may aid in breaking the momentum of depression."

   —*Joshua Ahles, PhD*, child and adolescent psychologist in independent
      practice in Issaquah, WA

"This is a *life-changing* workbook for any teen struggling with depression. Mezulis combines the most trusted, evidence-based treatment for depression with her deep understanding of the teen worldview to create a workbook that is engaging, practical, and profoundly attuned. If you are searching for a solution to relieve depression, this is it—your teen will feel better faster and carry that forward into lasting well-being."

   —*Katey Nicolai, PhD*, licensed clinical psychologist specializing in teen
      mental health, VP of clinical services at a teen mental health practice,
      and parent of two

"What a wonderful book! Mezulis is excellent at making clear what depression is, and provides a strong set of tools that are easy to apply in everyday life. The variety of research-based strategies are well explained and come with many opportunities for reflection and practice. Readers are encouraged to explore personal strengths and take action. This book is a must-read for all adolescents, including those not currently struggling with depression."

   —*Margot Bastin, PhD*, associate scientist at Oregon Research Institute,
      and research fellow at KU Leuven in Belgium

SIMPLE ACTIONS TO IMPROVE YOUR MOOD, BOOST MOTIVATION & BUILD THE LIFE YOU WANT

REVERSING THE SPIRAL OF DEPRESSION FOR TEENS

AMY MEZULIS, PHD

Instant Help Books
An Imprint of New Harbinger Publications, Inc.

Publisher's Note

NEW HARBINGER PUBLICATIONS is a registered trademark of New Harbinger Publications, Inc.

New Harbinger Publications is an employee-owned company.

New Harbinger Publications, Inc.
5720 Shattuck Avenue
Oakland, CA 94609
www.newharbinger.com

Cover design by Amy Shoup

Interior design by Tom Comitta

Acquired by Elizabeth Hollis Hansen

Edited by MC Calvi

Printed in the United States of America

26   25   24

10   9   8   7   6   5   4   3   2   1   First Printing

DEDICATION

For my girl gang, Anna and Elsie. And for all young people who face the hard parts of life head-on and come out stronger and wiser.

CONTENTS

FOREWORD

Depression in adolescence is a major public health problem in the United States. According to 2019 data, 16 percent of adolescents experienced a major depressive episode just in the past year (Daly 2022). That figure is roughly double what it was in 2009. Broken down by gender, 23 percent of adolescent girls and 9 percent of adolescent boys have experienced a major depressive episode. Depression is miserably common among adolescent girls, but we shouldn't forget that it afflicts boys, too.

In some sense, those numbers don't fully capture the magnitude of the problem. They only count depression in the past year, not across the teen's lifetime. So if the teen experienced major depression last year but not this year, they are not counted in the statistics. Also, the statistics only count major depression, not the milder forms, in which a person experiences some of the symptoms but not enough to meet the criteria for major depression. The number of adolescents who experience depression is a lot more than 16 percent.

Today, we have some highly effective treatments for depression, both in the form of "talk therapy" (psychotherapy) and drug therapy using antidepressants. But as a nation we aren't beginning to meet the need because there is a shortage of providers. University health services struggle to hire as many therapists as the demand calls for. Insurance coverage is often spotty. And sometimes there just isn't enough time for an overworked parent to take their teen to a provider once or twice a week.

What is needed is something that is inexpensive, widely available, and something you can do conveniently at home—a self-help workbook for teens experiencing depression. Enter Dr. Amy Mezulis's *Reversing the Spiral of Depression for Teens: Simple Actions to Improve Your Mood, Boost Motivation, and Build the Life You*

Want. It leaps over all those barriers that keep adolescents from getting treatment for their depression. It's just what the doctor ordered!

With hundreds of self-books out there, how do you pick the best one? First, you want an author with excellent credentials and expertise. A quick search on Amazon gave me a dozen or more hits of books on adolescent depression. Some of the books are written for parents and it's important for parents to have reliable information, but it's the teen who needs to become engaged and do the work. Among the ones written for teens, most were written by people with "MD" after their name. That is, they are medical doctors. They were trained in medical school. Some of them have a specialty in psychiatry, others in pediatrics. Some of my best friends are psychiatrists and pediatricians and they do wonderful work, but the problem is that they are not well-trained in "talk therapy." The approach they have been trained in is prescribing drugs such as antidepressants, which is not the experience needed for creating a workbook for adolescents. And then some of the authors have no initials after their name, meaning that they have no professional training in the field. Don't go with one of those. They may well be giving advice based on no scientific evidence, just their own hunches.

What you really want is an author with a PhD in clinical or counseling psychology, who has in-depth experience doing talk therapy with adolescents, who also knows the science of psychology. The science part is important because you always want to choose evidence-based treatments and approaches. In medicine, you want a drug that has been through clinical trials and has been approved. In psychology, you want approaches—treatments, interventions—that are evidence-based; that is, they have been subjected to scientific evaluation in a double-blind design with a control group, and the treatment yields better outcomes than the no-treatment control.

In psychology, we know a lot about adolescent depression, and we have lots of evidence-based treatments for it, as well as interventions to prevent it.

Dr. Amy Mezulis has precisely the credentials you want in an author. She has a PhD in clinical psychology from the highly ranked University of Wisconsin–Madison. She is an accomplished scientist who has published numerous research papers on adolescent depression. And she has conducted therapy with teens suffering from depression. In fact, she has served as the director of clinical training for PhD students at Seattle Pacific University, so she has trained therapists. Oh, and she has raised two daughters through adolescence. You can trust what she offers in this workbook.

—Janet Shibley Hyde, PhD
Professor Emerit of Psychology and Gender & Women's Studies
University of Wisconsin–Madison

PART 1

UNDERSTANDING DEPRESSION

Everybody gets sad. Everybody has a hard day once in a while. Everybody thinks "I suck" occasionally.

But what happens when these sad feelings, hard days, and negative thoughts aren't just once in a while? What happens when it starts to seem like you feel this way most of the time?

You might be depressed.

Depression is a lot more than "feeling sad." Depression is a mental health problem that can impact how you feel, how you're able to function in the world, and how your brain thinks and processes information. Depression is no fun, and it can be a really serious problem.

The first part of this workbook will help you understand what depression is, how it can show up differently for different people, and what can cause and maintain depression. Understanding your own symptoms and signs of depression is the first step toward feeling better.

CHAPTER 1

AM I DEPRESSED? WHAT DEPRESSION IS (AND WHAT IT ISN'T)

Sam is fourteen. He recently moved to a new town, and he hates it. All the kids have known each other since kindergarten, the high school is obsessed with its football team, and there's no music program. Sam used to love to play the trumpet in jazz band, he enjoyed musical theater, and had friends across lots of different classes and activities. Now Sam is angry all the time—at his parents for the move, at his old friends for not keeping in touch, at the new kids for their sports obsession. He doesn't see any point to keeping up his trumpet practice. Sam used to be a pretty decent student, but right now he can't find the motivation to do his homework or study. Sam is spending a lot of time alone in his room, scrolling through social media posts from his old friends and listening to music. Could Sam be depressed?

It's tough to be a teen. There's a lot of stress—school, friends, family, extracurriculars. There's a lot of change—expectations, relationships, your body. It's not surprising that your emotions are all over the place—from happy and confident one day to feeling overwhelmed, anxious, sad, or angry the next.

While it's normal to have lots of different emotions—to feel more moody, down, or sensitive than usual—for some teens these negative feelings last a long time and start to affect other areas of their lives. You might have trouble concentrating in school or when doing homework. You might not want to hang out with friends. You may find that things you used to like aren't fun anymore. You might find yourself doing things to escape those feelings, such as sleeping a lot, using alcohol or marijuana, or self-injury. You might start feeling like you'd be better off dead.

REFLECTION

How have you been feeling lately? Does anything in the previous paragraph describe you?

When those negative feelings start to take over your mood every day and start to affect other areas of your life, you might be depressed.

Depression is a significant mental health disorder. We call it a "mood disorder" because it definitely can affect your mood, but the truth is that depression affects *all* areas of your life.

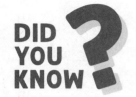
As many as one in five teens will have a depressive episode by age eighteen (Kessler et al. 2005).

The first step to knowing if you are depressed is to understand what depression is (and what it isn't). Depression can show up in lots of different ways; in fact, no two teens with depression will have exactly the same symptoms.

◎ DEPRESSION: MYTH VS. FACT

FACT CHECK: What do you know about depression? Circle whether each statement below is fact or myth.

Depressed teens can be more angry than sad.	Fact	Myth
Most depressed people cry a lot.	Fact	Myth
Depression can make it hard to sleep or eat enough.	Fact	Myth
Depression is only caused by stress.	Fact	Myth
Depression is only caused by genetics or biology.	Fact	Myth
Depression can affect motivation and concentration.	Fact	Myth
You should be able to just "power through" depression.	Fact	Myth

CHECKING THE FACTS!

Depressed teens can be more angry than sad.

FACT! Depression can make you feel sad or down, but it can also make you feel lots of other emotions—including anger! Many teens find that they feel irritable, on edge, or downright mad most of the time. They may find themselves lashing out at their parents or friends, or turn that anger toward themselves.

In fact, depression can also show up as emotions beyond sadness or anger. Feeling anxious is really common, as is feeling stressed or overwhelmed. And many teens report feeling "numb" or empty—like they don't feel anything at all.

Most depressed people cry a lot.

MYTH! Some depressed teens cry a lot. Others cry once in a while, and still others never cry at all. Since depression can show up as lots of different emotions, just because you don't cry doesn't mean you aren't depressed.

In fact, many teens report feeling "numb" or empty when they are depressed—like they can't cry even when they're sad.

Depression can make it hard to sleep or eat enough.

FACT! While we think of depression as a mood disorder, it can affect your body, sleep, and appetite. Some teens with depression find that they oversleep and can't ever seem to feel rested enough. Other teens find that they have a hard time falling asleep, or they wake up really early and can't get back to sleep. Similarly, some teens overeat as a way of coping with their emotions, while other teens find they have little or no appetite.

In fact, depression can affect your body in lots of ways. In addition to changes to sleep or appetite, depression can cause physical symptoms. Many teens find they have more headaches or stomachaches, or that their bodies feel "heavy" or weighed down.

Depression is caused only by stress or only by genetics.

MYTH! Depression is a complex disorder that is never caused by just one thing. In chapter 2, we'll go into more detail about the risk factors for depression, but the truth is that depression is usually the result of a lot of different things all adding up. Stress can certainly be one of those things, and we know that you're more likely to get depressed after major stressors such as loss, moving, changing schools, injury, and even trauma. And genetics (if anyone else in your family has been depressed) or biology (your hormones or brain chemistry) can definitely contribute as well.

In fact, most people find that their depression has more than one underlying cause. In the next chapter, you'll look more deeply into what might be contributing to your depression.

Depression can affect motivation and concentration.

FACT! Many teens find that it is very hard to keep up with schoolwork or their extracurricular activities when depressed. It can be very difficult to focus your attention on homework or find the motivation to care about grades, practice, or other goals you have (or had). Some of that is because it's hard to imagine a future in which you'd feel better enough to benefit from those activities. It's pretty hard to care about geometry homework or college applications when you're consumed with just getting through the day.

In fact, many kids find that they really don't care about things they used to find important, from grades to hobbies to friends and family. Even if they do still care, they can find it hard to muster the energy or focus to achieve the outcomes that used to come easily to them. As we'll learn about in chapter 3, the effect of depression on motivation and concentration is one of the "downward spirals" of depression. As you feel more depressed, you care less or can't concentrate as well, so your grades or performance often suffer, and then that makes you more depressed! It's a vicious cycle—but one we will learn how to interrupt in this book.

You should be able to just "power through" depression.

MYTH! Depression is a serious disorder. And most teens don't *want* to feel depressed—they'd like to feel better! If it was possible to just "power through" to cure depression, don't you think most people would do it?!?

In fact, the good news is that there are a lot of things you can do to treat your depression and start feeling better right now. There are easy-to-learn and easy-to-implement ways to manage stress better, improve focus and motivation, and build more positive emotions into your life. And doing these things will help you battle your own depression and become the person you want to be.

Because depression is different for each person, knowing how depression shows up for *you* is the first step in making the most of this workbook. Some of the strategies we'll learn won't be helpful to you—but others may be super helpful. By understanding your own depression better, you'll be able to choose and practice the strategies that can help you the most.

⊚ SELF-DISCOVERY: AM I DEPRESSED?

Have you been noticing any of these symptoms in the last two weeks? Check all that apply to you.

AM I DEPRESSED?

Check Your Symptoms

1	I'm sad a lot.	
	I can't feel happy.	
	I get annoyed easily.	
2	I don't have any energy.	
	I can't get motivated to do things.	
	I avoid talking to people.	
3	It's hard to concentrate.	
	I think I'm a failure.	
	I think about suicide or what it would be like to not be here anymore.	
4	My sleep has changed (I sleep too much or can't sleep).	
	I often have stomachaches or headaches.	
	My eating has changed (I eat too much or have no appetite).	

NOW, COUNT UP YOUR CHECKS.

0-3: You are probably not depressed. However, we all have times when we feel better and worse. Take a look at the items you checked—they may be areas you want to work on.

4-5: You might be depressed. There are some areas of your life in which you are struggling, and you may benefit from working to improve in these areas.

6 OR MORE: You are likely depressed. There are several areas of your life in which you are struggling, and you would likely benefit from working to improve in these areas.

NOTE: This checklist is a great starting point for understanding your emotions, thoughts, behaviors, and physical symptoms (Kroenke et al. 1999). But only a medical provider using a full assessment can determine if you have a clinical diagnosis.

DIGGING DEEPER

Depression has many features. It affects how we feel, how we behave, how we think, and how our bodies work. There are many different ways that depression shows up. Some teens with depression, like Sam, may feel angry, have low motivation, and isolate themselves. Others may feel overwhelmed, have trouble sleeping and concentrating, and have thoughts about hurting themselves. If you are depressed, it is very important to know how depression affects you personally.

DEPRESSION AND YOU: How does depression affect the way you feel, behave, think, and how your body works?

If you look at the chart of depression symptoms in the previous section, you'll see they are clustered by number (1, 2, 3, 4).

Each set of symptoms relates to one area of your life that depression can impact.

 **HOW YOU FEEL:** Depression can cause sadness, but it can also make it hard to feel positive emotions (joy, happiness, love) and easy to feel other negative emotions (irritability, anxiety, overwhelmed). Notice which feelings you marked: Did that include sadness? Low happiness? Irritability?

 **HOW YOU BEHAVE:** Depression can affect energy and motivation, making it difficult to function in daily life. You may find that you have little energy for schoolwork, extracurriculars, or your friends. Notice which behaviors you marked in this section—low energy, low motivation, or social avoidance.

 HOW YOU THINK: Depression can impact how you think about yourself and the world. It is common to have trouble concentrating, to have a lot of negative thoughts about yourself, and even to start having thoughts of death, self-harm, or suicide. Notice what depression thoughts you marked in this section.

HOW YOUR BODY WORKS: Depression can directly show up in physical symptoms, such as noticing more headaches, stomachaches, or muscle aches. It can also affect your biorhythms, such as your eating and sleeping patterns. Notice how depression has been showing up in your body.

REFLECTION
REFLECTION

How does depression affect your emotions, behaviors, thoughts, and body? Draw your depression below.

I THINK I'M DEPRESSED. NOW WHAT?

Some teens with depression need more help than a workbook can offer. If you are self-injuring or have seriously considered suicide, if you have been skipping school or using substances, or if you feel hopeless that you can ever feel better, please get help right away. You can ask a parent, teacher, or other trusted adult for help, or you can call or text the nationwide Suicide and Crisis Lifeline at 9-8-8.

Many teens with depression can feel better by doing the activities in this workbook. Step by step, this book can help you feel better, build motivation, and create the happier, nondepressed life you want to live.

Let's get started!

CHAPTER 2

UNDERSTANDING DEPRESSION: RISK FACTORS AND STRESS

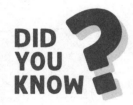 Did you know that 70 percent of depression episodes are triggered by a stressful life event (Monroe and Harkness 2005)?

It's true! While it's not totally fair to say that stress causes depression, it is fair to say that stress makes it much more likely we could get depressed.

Not everyone gets depressed when things are stressful, and not all stressful events cause depression. But there *is* a clear link between stress and depression. The more stress you have to handle, the more likely it is you'll get overwhelmed and become depressed.

WHAT DO WE MEAN BY "STRESS"?

When we think about stress, it is helpful to think about two different kinds of stress. The first is *daily stress*—these are the relatively common day-to-day hassles, pressures, and challenges that most of us have to deal with. Daily stress is pretty unavoidable, but everyone has different amounts to deal with at different times of their life.

The second is *major stress*—these are less common but bigger and more impactful life events. Not everyone is dealing with major life stress, but most of us will have to face these kinds of major events at some point in our lives.

What kinds of stress are you facing right now?

⊚ SELF-DISCOVERY: SOURCES OF STRESS

Which of the following common sources of daily stress are you dealing with right now? Circle all of the stressors you've been struggling with.

MY DAILY SOURCES OF STRESS

Homework/ school	Friend drama/ conflict	Family conflict	Divorce
Sports	Money	Health problems	Sibling conflict
Dating/ romantic relationships	College planning	Work	Extra-curriculars
Chores	Body image	Friends with mental health problems	Family with mental health problems

In addition to daily stress, are you also coping with any of the following types of major stress? Circle all of the things you're struggling with below.

MY MAJOR SOURCES OF STRESS

Car accident	Sexual abuse or assault	Loss of a loved one
Chronic health condition	Homelessness or food insecurity	Natural disaster (fire, tornado, earthquake)
Trauma	Major injury or illness	Recent move
Discrimination or harassment	Loved one with major health concern	School shooting or community trauma

One of the first steps of healing your depression is figuring out what you need to heal from. Now that you've done this exercise, you should have a better idea of what you're facing. These stressors—and more—really are very common and understandable things to struggle with. So please show yourself compassion as you work through this book.

As we know, stress is one of the major factors in depression. However, there are also several other types of *risk factors* for depression to consider. Let's explore them now.

WHAT'S A "RISK FACTOR"?

Risk factors are things that increase your risk of getting depressed when stressful things happen. Some risk factors are outside your control (like genetics), but others are inside your control (like your coping strategies or thinking styles). Understanding your own risk factors can help you figure out your personal level of risk for depression, as well as ways you might decrease your risk in the future.

Risk Factors for Depression

GENETICS: Do you have a family history of depression? If so, you may have a genetic predisposition to depression. We know that depression runs in families, and that it seems to be related to how other mental health problems run in families (such as substance use and anxiety). But we don't know exactly how genetic risk works—there is no one gene for depression. Research suggests that there are many genes that may increase the risk for depression, but no one gene that causes it (Dunn et al. 2015).

REFLECTION *Do others in your family struggle with depression?*
REFLECTION

_____

_____

_____

_____

HORMONES: While a lot of people may say that puberty causes depression, the truth is much more complicated. During the years around puberty (typically around ages eleven to fourteen for girls and thirteen to sixteen for boys), your body's complex chemistry is changing rapidly. Hormones do affect how sensitive you might be to stress, how moody or irritable you are, your sleep, and your energy levels—all things that might make it harder to handle stress well. So, while hormones don't directly cause depression, the hormone changes that most teens are dealing with definitely make it harder to handle stress, which can make you more likely to get depression.

BODY CHEMISTRY: Have you ever noticed that when something unexpected or stressful happens, your body reacts? Your heart may race, your stomach might flip over, you may find that you get a little sweaty or shaky. This is because your nervous system, like everyone's, is set up to react to stressful events with a whole set of biochemical reactions that are meant to help you handle the situation. This "fight-or-flight" response is super handy when there's a major threat (imagine a bear chasing you!). But it turns out that every body is different—and some of us have bodies that react to pretty small stressors as if they are a bear chasing us. Is that you? Are you someone whose heart races easily, whose stomach is easily upset from stress, or who can't sleep when you're stressed out? If so, you might have a body that is more reactive to stress than other kids' bodies, and this can put you at increased risk for depression.

REFLECTION   *Does your body react strongly to stress?*

_____

_____

_____

COPING STRATEGIES: Coping strategies are the ways you've learned to handle stress, from things you may have been taught to how you've observed others handle stress. Some of our learned coping strategies are super helpful and effective, but other learned coping strategies are less than helpful and can make things worse. Most of us have a mix of helpful and not-so-helpful coping strategies (and you'll have the chance to do a self-check on your coping in chapter 7). The good news? You can learn more effective coping skills that can lower your risk for depression.

Common Coping Strategies

Helpful Coping Strategies	Not-So-Helpful Coping Strategies
Asking for help	Withdrawing
Problem solving	Avoiding or ignoring problem
Taking a break until calm	Acting out on negative emotions
Positive self-talk	Self-blame or negative self-talk
Optimism	Hopelessness

 **REFLECTION** *Do you recognize any of your own coping styles from this list?*

_____

_____

_____

THINKING STYLES: Let's imagine that you have a big audition coming up, but the night before, you get the stomach flu and can't attend. You end up getting a very minor role and not the major role you'd prepared for. What do you find yourself thinking? Maybe something like, "Life is so unfair. Nothing good ever happens for me. There's no point in even taking the minor role; I should just quit." Or maybe, you think to yourself, "What rotten timing. I'm so disappointed, but these things happen. I'll do the best I can in my small role and hopefully next time things will go better."

It turns out that when stressful stuff happens, it matters a lot how we think—both about the stress and about ourselves. While nearly everyone gets upset, disappointed, sad, or anxious when stress happens, people who can find a way to think positively about it are less likely to get depressed than people who think negative, pessimistic, or self-critical thoughts.

Life is so unfair. Nothing good ever happens for me. There's no point in even taking the minor role; I should just quit.

What rotten timing. I'm so disappointed, but these things happen. I'll do the best I can in my small role and hopefully next time things will go better.

REMEMBER! There is *no one explanation* for depression, and no one risk factor can perfectly predict who gets depressed and who doesn't. Most people with depression have a mix of a few risk factors, plus stressful life events that they are coping with. It's best to think of risk factors and stress as weights that add up on a scale—each weight might only move the scale a little, but the more weights you have, the more likely you are to tip the scale into depression.

CHAPTER 3

THE DOWNWARD SPIRAL
OF DEPRESSION

Have you ever watched one of those cartoons showing a snowball rolling down a hill, getting bigger and bigger and bigger until it rolls over everything in its path?

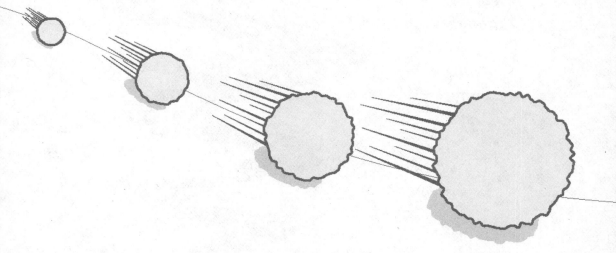

Depression is like that—what seems to make us start feeling depressed is sometimes so small we don't even notice it. But depression is a sneaky snowball—it gains size and momentum very quickly, until all of a sudden, your depression snowball has rolled right over you.

In fact, we have a term for this: the downward spiral of depression.

WHAT IS THE DOWNWARD SPIRAL OF DEPRESSION?

The downward spiral is the idea that one stressful event can trigger a whole series of reactions that "spiral" down, until what was one bad mood or one bad day has turned into a full-blown depressive episode. Let's check it out.

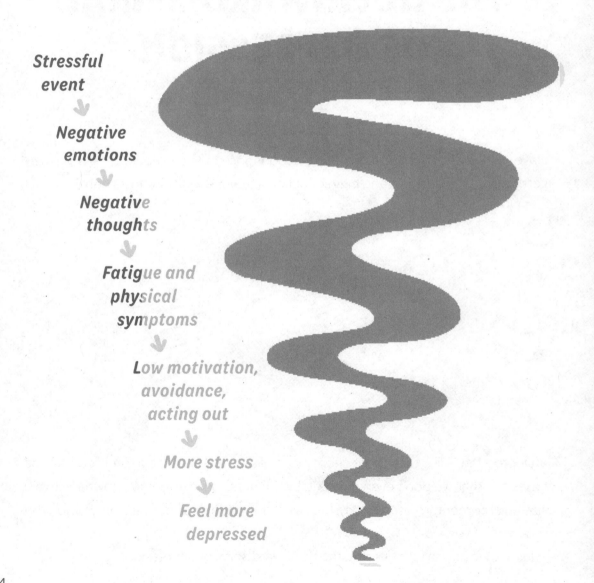

Stressful event

Negative emotions

Negative thoughts

Fatigue and physical symptoms

Low motivation, avoidance, acting out

More stress

Feel more depressed

STRESSFUL EVENT

A typical downward spiral often starts with stress. This could be something major (like losing someone you love) or something smaller that matters to you (like not doing well on a test or not getting a role in the school play).

NEGATIVE EMOTIONS

It's normal that when we're stressed, we feel upset, sad, anxious, or angry. There's nothing wrong with negative emotions themselves—they tell us there's something wrong, after all. But for some of us, those negative feelings kick off a larger set of unhelpful thoughts and behaviors.

NEGATIVE THOUGHTS

If we respond to negative emotions with negative thoughts, we usually end up feeling worse. Negative thoughts may be things like "It's all my fault" (self-blame) or "Everything always goes wrong for me" (pessimism) or "There's nothing I can do" (hopelessness).

FATIGUE AND PHYSICAL SYMPTOMS

When we have a lot of negative thoughts and feelings swirling around inside us, it can show up as trouble sleeping, fatigue, stomachaches, and headaches. Feeling bad can make it hard to do anything.

LOW MOTIVATION, AVOIDANCE, ACTING OUT

When we aren't feeling good emotionally or physically, it's pretty common to find it hard to get anything done. You might oversleep and not finish your homework (low motivation). You might not want to hang out with your friends (avoidance). You may get irritable or turn to substances or self-injury to relieve the pain (acting out). While in the short term, these behaviors seem to help, they often just create more problems.

MORE STRESS

If you're not getting schoolwork done, you're avoiding friends or activities, or you're using substances, odds are that more stressful things have started to happen. Maybe your grades are dropping, you feel disconnected from your peers, or you have conflicts with parents or others. More stress means more spiraling.

FEEL MORE DEPRESSED

As things in your life increasingly feel out of control, odds are that you will feel increasingly out of control, too. Your negative thoughts and feelings just get stronger and stronger until they turn into full-blown depression.

Remember the story of Sam from chapter 1? The kid who had to change towns in the middle of high school and hates his new town? Let's look at Sam's downward spiral of depression.

SAM'S DOWNWARD SPIRAL

Moved to new school

Feels down and angry

Thinks "I'll never be happy here"

Has no energy for or interest in doing things

Doesn't join activities; stops doing homework

Is isolated; grades dropping; parents frustrated

Gets more depressed

⊚ SELF-DISCOVERY: WHAT IS YOUR DEPRESSION SPIRAL?

Reflect a little on how you got to feeling the way you do now. It was probably a lot of things that added up. It is okay if you can't fit something in every box, but take a look at what happens for you, and then try to fill out your own version of the depression spiral below. This will give us some good idea how to get you out of this depression spiral.

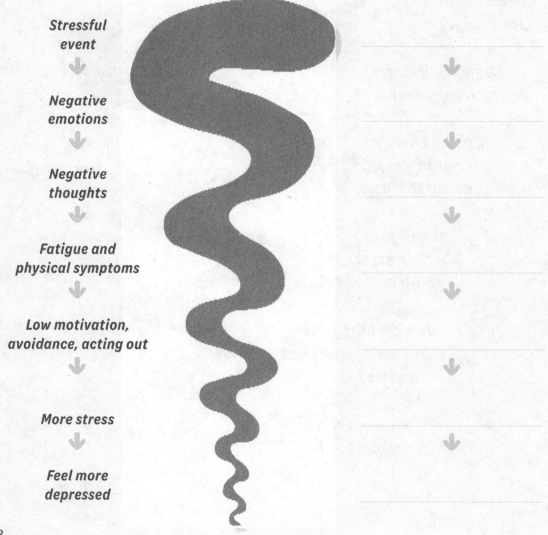

Stressful event
⬇
Negative emotions
⬇
Negative thoughts
⬇
Fatigue and physical symptoms
⬇
Low motivation, avoidance, acting out
⬇
More stress
⬇
Feel more depressed

Everyone's depression spiral will look a little different. Some teens notice they have a lot of negative thoughts when stressed. Others struggle with sleep and fatigue more than negative thoughts. Still others sleep fine but find they have no motivation for school or activities.

But no matter what *your* depression spiral looks like, it gives us some good ideas where to start to interrupt that spiral. This workbook will help you reverse that downward spiral with small, daily changes that improve mood, improve motivation, and help you build the life you want to live.

CHAPTER 4

REVERSE THE SPIRAL: HOW DAILY CHANGES CAN BEAT DEPRESSION

Here's the good news: you *can* feel better! This step-by-step guide can help you interrupt the downward spiral of depression and even reverse it, so you can get back to feeling yourself again.

There are a lot of small activities in this workbook. Since every person is different and everyone's depression is different, not all of the strategies will work for you. You'll try them out, take what helps, and leave the rest.

The activities are organized into three sections:

1. **FEEL BETTER:** You can't make important changes to your life or dig your way out of the hole created by your depression while you feel so bad. So, first up are activities that improve mood quickly so that you feel a bit better—things like getting more active and solving sleep problems. Next up is a deep dive into your negative thinking styles, followed by coping skills to help you handle stress better. Armed with these skills, you'll see your mood get a little better day by day.

2. **IMPROVE MOTIVATION:** With your mood improving a bit, we'll be able to tackle motivation. One of the key parts of the depression spiral is how mood impacts motivation and concentration. When we don't feel motivated or can't concentrate, it is hard to get things done (like homework, chores, or making plans). And when we don't get things done, stuff piles up, and we just feel more overwhelmed—that depression spiral is hard at work! To reverse that spiral, we have to get your motivation back. There is a lot of new research in the field of neuroscience (basically, how the brain works) on what can help rebuild motivation. We'll learn some of these strategies and put them to practice to help you dig out of your depression hole.

3. **BUILD THE LIFE YOU WANT TO LIVE:** One of the ways we protect ourselves from falling back into depression again is by building a strong set of internal skills that make us resilient to stress. These are skills like knowing your own strengths to build self-esteem, using positive self-talk and gratitude to build positive thinking skills, and developing social connections to build a support network. In this section, we'll actually reverse that downward spiral and turn it into an upward spiral where you build the life you want to live!

Ready to get started? Let's reverse that depression spiral and get you feeling better!

PART 2

FEEL BETTER

The good news is that, now that you've started to really understand your own depression, you've taken the first step toward feeling better. Now that you know what sets off your depression and makes you start to spiral, you can find places to make changes.

Thankfully, it turns out that even small changes are enough to stop that downward spiral and help you start to feel better. So, in part 2 of this book, we're going to talk about what those changes are, which ones will help you the most, and how to make them.

Specifically, we're going to talk about three different types of action you can take to start recovering from depression right now. The first two types of action will help your body feel and function better by getting you moving more and improving your sleep. The last one, on the other hand, will help your brain function better by improving how you handle stress and changing the negative thinking patterns you've gotten stuck in.

Let's get started on feeling better!

CHAPTER 5

GET MOVING

Depression often causes us to feel tired, have low energy, and lack motivation. That can make it hard to do even basic things like get exercise. When all our brain and body want to do is watch videos or nap, it can be hard to get moving. We're just so tired—and keep feeling like if we just get enough rest, we'll finally have the energy or desire to do more.

That's tricky, though, because the downward spiral of depression is at work. As it turns out, the less exercise or movement we get, the *less* energy we have. The less energy we have, the harder it is to get moving. And so on... The spiral is hard at work keeping us depressed.

The way to interrupt this downward spiral is to get moving. As in, literally move your body. Even if you don't feel like it. Even if you're tired. Even if you don't want to. Study after study shows that physical activity improves mood. So, let's get moving!

Exercise helps you cope with stress better! It decreases the stress hormone cortisol and increases the coping hormone norepinephrine (Caplin et al. 2021).

First off, what counts as physical activity? For the purposes of improving mood, we're interested in anything that involves moving your body. It doesn't have to be a big exercise routine or becoming a gym rat or learning a new sport. Some common examples are:

- Walking, which includes walking to and from classes, walking your dog, and planned walks or hikes. If you use a smartphone or smart watch, you probably can look at your step count on a typical school day and a typical weekend day. Fifteen minutes of moderate walking should be about two thousand steps.

- Structured class or practice, including PE class, any organized sports practice, or a class at a gym or fitness studio.

- Strength training using body weight, free weights, machines, or bands.

- Activities such as biking, skateboarding, skiing, or surfing.

- Dancing, whether in a class, on your own, or using your hairbrush as a microphone.

- Yoga, Pilates, or similar types of exercise—you can find plenty of videos about how to practice these online.

When fitness tracking devices first came on the market, there was a lot of buzz about needing to get 10,000 steps a day. That's a *lot* of steps! There's actually very little science to this number. Healthy step goals can be anywhere from 2,000 to 7,500 steps a day, depending on factors such as your age and how much you already walk (Paulch et al. 2022). As we'll discuss below, setting realistic movement goals is much more important than any absolute number.

Now, let's be practical: If you're already a high-level athlete—a soccer player or elite swimmer or something—chances are that you get plenty of exercise. You may want to skip ahead to the next chapter and focus on other skills to improve your depression.

But if you're like most teens with depression, and you know you're probably not getting enough physical activity, keep reading.

⊚ SELF-DISCOVERY: MOVEMENT YOU ENJOY

The best way to get moving is to identify physical activities that (1) you think you might enjoy, and (2) are available to you. Let's see if we can find out what those are.

What kind of movement do you enjoy? Movement comes in many different forms, and the most important thing is choosing a form of movement that feels genuine to you. Circle all the activities that you enjoy below. For right now, don't worry about if you can easily do them—just circle ones you think you might like.

School gym/fitness center	Taking PE/fitness at school	Downhill skiing
Snowboarding	Cross-country skiing	Snowshoeing
Local gym/fitness center	Walking	Hiking
Running	Paddleboarding	Waterskiing
Basketball	Baseball/softball	Soccer
Swimming	Dancing	Home workouts (e.g. using videos)
Yoga	Karate/martial arts	Stretching

DID WE MISS ONE THAT YOU LOVE?
WRITE OTHER OPTIONS HERE:

_____

What's available to you? Movement can take many different forms depending on what is easily available to you based on cost, location, and time. You might be interested in taking a yoga class or joining a local gym, but your budget doesn't allow you to. You might love being outside, but you don't have a car or other way to get to hiking trails. You might want to go for long runs, but your schedule doesn't have much room during the day time and it isn't safe to run at night.

Pick three activities from the list above and write down a practical, available way for you to engage in it. You might have to get a little creative about how (on your own, video, class...), when (after school, weekends...), and where (home, neighborhood, gym or community center, park, school track...).

WHAT I LIKE TO DO	HOW	WHEN	WHERE
Take walks	On my own	Weekend afternoons	Around neighborhood or at the school track

MAKE A PLAN

In chapter 10, we're going to talk in more detail about setting SMART goals. But for now, it is important to set a reasonable goal that makes sense for you. A good movement goal for you, to help with your depression, will not necessarily be a good movement goal for anyone else—and vice versa.

A good goal should build from where you're starting. Do an inventory of your current movement—including the incidental movement that comes from walking to and from classes or activities. Look at the statements below and circle the one that best describes you right now.

I spend most of my time sitting or lying down. My daily life doesn't include much walking or activity.

I walk when I need to (to and from class or the car) but otherwise don't do any planned movement.

My daily life includes a fair bit of incidental activity—I walk a lot to and from classes or to and from home, and I have activities that require movement (e.g., a job or chores that include lifting or moving things).

I do some intentional movement one or two times a week (sports practice, class, or self-guided activity).

I do some intentional movement three or four times a week (sports practice, class, or self-guided activity).

I do some intentional movement five or more times a week (sports practice, class, or self-guided activity).

Unless you're already at three or more days of intentional movement per week, it might help your mood to get moving. Let's work on setting a reasonable goal that just extends where you are right now.

EXAMPLE: Jesse does online school from home and otherwise spends most of her time playing video games in her room. She's not a huge fan of "exercise" and feels tired and low energy all the time. She has no interest in joining a sport or going to a gym or community center. However, she doesn't mind walking if the weather is decent, and she is willing to try small workouts in her bedroom.

JESSE'S MOVEMENT GOAL: Start with one ten-minute walk each weekend in her neighborhood. She'll also look for five-to-ten-minute home workout videos that can be done in her room and don't require any equipment.

EXAMPLE: Suresh used to enjoy running and in fact did middle school track. He's not sure about joining the high school track team just yet. Suresh still has his running shoes, though, and his dog needs more exercise. He lives near a park that has safe, paved running trails.

SURESH'S MOVEMENT GOAL: Suresh will take his dog for runs at the park twice a week after school. He used to be able to run two miles easily, but for now he'll start with running one mile and then walking to cool down.

◎ MY GET MOVING PLAN

Look back at the activities you wrote down as being available to you. Now, make a plan for this week that makes sense with your schedule.

WHAT I LIKE TO DO	HOW	WHEN	WHERE
Take walks	On my own	Weekend afternoons	Around neighborhood or at the school track

MY PLAN: I'm going to take a walk on Wednesday after school. I will do two laps around my street.

WHAT I LIKE TO DO	HOW	WHEN	WHERE

MY PLAN:

All that said, variety is the spice of life. So let's come up with some other options for movement or activities you can do on weeks you can't manage that plan—or just really want to do something else!

WHAT I LIKE TO DO	HOW	WHEN	WHERE

MY PLAN: _____

_____

_____

CHAPTER 6

REST IS BEST

Depression can really mess with our sleep. Sometimes we feel so tired all the time that all we want to do is sleep. Before we know it, we're sleeping ten to twelve hours a night and taking a nap every day.

On the other hand, sometimes we can't sleep. Depression often causes sleep disruption, including difficulty falling asleep, difficulty staying asleep, or waking up early and not being able to get back to sleep.

Sleep is tricky, because it is an important part of the depression spiral. When we're depressed, we have sleep problems, but sleep problems (both oversleeping and not sleeping enough) often make us feel more depressed. Sleeping too much can make us feel constantly sluggish and tired, because we don't have enough opportunity to do things that give us energy or a feeling of accomplishment. Sleeping too little can make us feel irritable, anxious, and overwhelmed, because we're not getting enough rest to take on the day effectively.

Getting your sleep into a healthy, sustainable pattern can really improve your mood.

Teens need eight to ten hours of sleep per night to function at their best (Paruthi et al. 2016)!

First up, let's take a good inventory of your current sleep patterns.

◎ SLEEP PATTERN INVENTORY

Think back on your sleep over the last week. Let's look at your sleep during the weekdays (usually Monday through Friday) and during the weekend (Saturday and Sunday).

TYPICAL WEEKDAY (MONDAY TO FRIDAY)

What time I go to bed: _____

How long it takes me to fall asleep (circle one):

> Less than fifteen minutes
>
> Fifteen to thirty minutes
>
> Thirty to sixty minutes
>
> More than one hour

What time I set my alarm for/what time I plan to get up: _____

What time I actually get up: _____

I'd describe my sleep as:

> _____ Deep: Once I'm out, I'm out.
>
> _____ Light: I feel like I'm never fully asleep.
>
> _____ Disrupted: I sleep, but I wake often or have disturbing dreams.

Do you take naps? (Circle one)

Often

Sometimes

Never

TYPICAL WEEKEND (SATURDAY AND SUNDAY)

What time I go to bed: _____

How long it takes me to fall asleep (circle one):

Less than fifteen minutes

Fifteen to thirty minutes

Thirty to sixty minutes

More than one hour

What time I set my alarm for/what time I plan to get up: _____

What time I actually get up: _____

I'd describe my sleep as:

_____ Deep: Once I'm out, I'm out.

_____ Light: I feel like I'm never fully asleep.

_____ Disrupted: I sleep, but I wake often or have disturbing dreams.

Do you take naps? (Circle one)

Often

Sometimes

Never

Now look at the inventory you just completed and check all that apply to you below:

MY SLEEP INVENTORY

SLEEP BEHAVIOR	MOST DAYS	WEEKDAYS ONLY	WEEKENDS ONLY
I get less than seven hours of sleep.			
I get more than ten hours of sleep.			
It takes me more than one hour to fall asleep.			
My sleep is disrupted.			
It is hard for me to get up in the morning.			
I take naps.			

 *How many boxes did you check? Are your weekdays and weekends different?*

Many teens find that their sleep patterns are really different on school days/week-days than on weekends or holidays. And many depressed teens find that they have sleep problems—sleeping too little, sleeping too much, or needing naps to get through the day.

If this is you, keep reading! We're going to work on improving your sleep!

BASICS OF GOOD SLEEP

Have you ever been really, really tired but not able to sleep? It's super frustrating but also super common.

That's because sleep is a behavior. We don't sleep simply because we're tired. It turns out that we often simply sleep when our body expects to sleep. Although the body does have some natural biorhythms, it has an amazing ability to shift sleep patterns based on what we teach it to do. This is great news for improving sleep—we can help our body relearn healthy sleep habits!

Here are the core principles of good sleep:

SAME TIME, SAME PLACE: The body likes to anticipate a regular pattern of being awake and being tired and going to sleep. Going to bed at about the same time and waking up at about the same time most days helps train the body to be tired at bedtime and awake at wake time.

Hey! I like to sleep in on the weekends and I'm so tired after getting up early during the week—are you telling me I can't sleep in??? No, it's okay to sleep in sometimes. Ideally, we'd find a way to get more sleep during the week, but if you need to "catch up" on the weekends, that's okay. If you can, though, try to go to bed and wake up no more than one and a half to two hours later than usual. It's still extra sleep, but doesn't disrupt your sleep pattern so much.

HAVE A SLEEP ROUTINE: The body and brain need to wind down for sleep, and having a sleep routine is a great way to prompt your brain to realize that it is sleep time. Sleep routines can include changing clothes, washing face, brushing teeth, stretching, listening to quiet music, even reading. The important things are to (1) get off screens, and (2) do the same things, preferably in the same order, every night before bed.

SAVE YOUR BED FOR SLEEPING: We want your brain to associate your bed with sleep, not with doing homework, playing video games, or watching videos. If you're doing those things in your bedroom, try doing them while sitting on the floor or at your desk instead.

SET YOURSELF UP FOR SUCCESS: Things that keep you awake—especially caffeinated drinks—are not going to help you sleep! It takes five to six hours for the effects of caffeine to wear off. That means you need to stop drinking caffeinated beverages at least six hours before bedtime (National Institutes of Health 2020)!

DON'T LAY IN BED NOT SLEEPING: Since sleep is a behavior, if we lay in bed not sleeping then we're training our brain that bed is for...not sleeping. If you've been in bed trying to sleep for twenty minutes and are still awake, get out of bed for ten minutes. Repeat some or all of your sleep routine and try again.

MINIMIZE NAPPING: I know—sad, right? Naps are so appealing, especially when you haven't been sleeping well and are so tired. But naps can disrupt our circadian rhythm, making it harder to fall asleep that night (yes, even if we're still tired). Research shows that short naps (under thirty minutes) in the early afternoon (before three o'clock) don't disrupt sleep—but longer naps later in the day can interfere with your nighttime sleep.

The good news is, you can change your behavior to improve your sleep! Let's get started on sleeping better.

⊚ MY BETTER SLEEP PLAN

Think about what you've learned about your sleep so far this chapter. When we are well-rested, we focus better, handle stress better, have more energy, and feel calmer.

There are a lot of things that interfere with getting enough sleep. Which of the following apply to you? (Circle all that apply.)

Being on phone right before bed

Feeling stressed

Having caffeine in the afternoon

Having a lot of homework

Taking naps

Sleeping in on weekends

Look at the ones you circled. Pick *one* sleep barrier you'd like to work on to improve your sleep, and set a better sleep goal for this week.

Here are some examples of other sleep goals to help with these barriers. Circle *one* goal (or come up with your own!) and plan to stick to it for the next week.

Go to bed at the same time.

No naps after 3 p.m.

Get out of bed if I'm not sleeping.

Put my phone away before bed.

No caffeine after 3 p.m.

Follow a sleep routine.

Example

MY SLEEP BARRIER: I'm so tired after school that I end up taking a nap, and then I'm awake until two in the morning.

BETTER SLEEP GOAL: This week I'm going to not take a nap after school. If I'm really tired, I'll go to bed earlier that night.

My Better Sleep Plan

MY SLEEP BARRIER:

_____

_____

BETTER SLEEP GOAL:

_____

_____

◉ HOW TO WIND DOWN

One common sleep problem is difficulty falling asleep. Here are some strategies to calm down before sleep:

Deep breathing

Read a book

Journal

Meditate/mindfulness

Take a warm bath

Stretch

What are three things you can do before bed to calm your mind and body for sleep?

1. _____

2. _____

3. _____

IDEA! Creating a bedtime routine that helps you get ready for sleep can help a lot. About fifteen minutes before you want to go to sleep, make time for your hygiene routine (brushing teeth, etc.), turn your phone off, and do a quiet activity.

You're on your way to better sleep! Sweet dreams!

CHAPTER 7

MANAGE STRESS

As we talked about in chapter 2, stress is a part of what can cause depression. This is especially true if you don't have good ways to manage the stress in your life.

Our goal in life is not to avoid stress—many forms of stress are hard to avoid. Our goal is to be able to handle stress with good coping skills, so we can get through the hard times without making things worse.

Before we dig deeper into what serves as a good coping strategy for managing stress, let's take stock of what kinds of stress management skills you already have. This will help you evaluate where you already have strong, helpful coping skills, and where you can try to develop better ones.

◎ COPING SKILLS INVENTORY

Think about how you usually act when something stressful happens. Then, using this chart (Tobin et al. 1989), circle all the things that you often do when you're stressed, overwhelmed, or faced with a difficult problem:

COPING SKILLS INVENTORY

1	2	3	4	5
Talk to a friend about it	Do an art project, cook, or read	Journal about the situation	Break the problem down into parts	Take a long nap
Ask for help from some-one you trust	Exercise or take a walk	Try to talk positively to yourself about it	Make a to-do list for the problem	Play games, watch TV, or scroll social media
Discuss with a parent, teach-er, or another adult	Listen to music	List things you're grateful for	Reach out to get questions answered	Hide emotions and pretend to be okay
Connect with friends (text, etc.)	Play with your pet	Focus on changing your negative thoughts	Brainstorm possible solutions	Avoid thinking about it
Do some-thing fun with friends or family	Clean or organize	Try to think about it an-other way	Ask people with similar problems for help	Procrastinate
Attend a sup-port group or affinity group	Go outside or into nature	Come up with affirmations for yourself about the situation	Research potential strategies	Eat your feelings
Call a support line	Take a bath	Focus your attention on good things in your life	Set goals to change the situation	Use substanc-es or engage in self-harm

Now look down each column (1, 2, 3, 4, 5) and count how many items in each column you circled. The total should be from 0 (the lowest) to 7 (the highest) in each column.

UNPACKING YOUR COPING INVENTORY

Each column above represents one common stress management style.
Let's look deeper into each column.

Social Support (Column 1)

Social support is the ability to reach out to others when stressed and ask for support, help, or simply someone to spend time with. *Social support is a helpful coping strategy!*

How many social support coping skills did you circle?

0-3: This is an area of growth for you! In this workbook, we'll work on how to strengthen social support networks.

4-5: You are pretty good at using social support but could strengthen this skill.

6 OR MORE: This is an area of strength for you!

Distraction (Column 2)

Distraction is the ability to think about or do something else when stressed, so that you're not just dwelling on the problem. Distraction helps us calm down when upset, and can stop the cycle of negative thoughts. While it doesn't necessarily solve the immediate situation, *distraction is a helpful coping strategy* in the short term.

How many distraction skills did you circle?

0-3: This is an area of growth for you! In this workbook, we'll work on how to build more fun, distracting activities into your life.

4-5: You are pretty good at using distraction but could strengthen this skill.

6 OR MORE: This is an area of strength for you!

Reframing (Column 3)

Reframing is the ability to think about the problem in a new, more positive way. That can mean using some self-talk to motivate yourself or trying to see the good even in a difficult situation. Reframing helps us turn negative, hopeless thoughts into more positive, hopeful ones. *Reframing is a helpful coping strategy!*

How many reframing skills did you circle?

0-3: This is an area of growth for you! In this workbook, we'll work on how to recognize and reframe negative thoughts.

4-5: You are pretty good at using reframing but could strengthen this skill.

6 OR MORE: This is an area of strength for you!

Problem Solving (Column 4)

Problem solving is the ability to look at a stressful situation or problem and try to find a way to change it. Problem solving is a very active stress coping skill, and can include breaking the problem down into parts, gathering information, generating solutions, and then acting on them. While not all stressful situations have solutions, when there is a problem that can be solved, *problem solving is a helpful coping strategy.*

0-3: This is an area of growth for you! In this workbook, we'll work on how to focus on a problem and generate goals to resolve it.

4-5: You are pretty good at using problem solving but could strengthen this skill.

6 OR MORE: This is an area of strength for you!

Avoidance Coping (Column 5)

Avoidance coping is a passive way of trying to pretend that the stressful situation or problem isn't there, or trying to avoid feeling upset, thinking about it, or working to improve the situation. While none of us wants to think about stress any more than we have to, avoidance tends to make us feel worse and doesn't give us the opportunity to improve the situation. As a result, *avoidance is an unhelpful coping strategy*.

0-3: Good job! You don't rely too much on avoidance coping when stressed.

4-5: You are pretty good at using more helpful coping strategies but still use avoidance sometimes.

6 OR MORE: You might default to avoidance coping when you're feeling stressed or overwhelmed. Don't worry, this is probably because you don't have enough helpful coping strategies to rely on. Across this workbook you'll learn some new coping skills that will help you rely less on avoidance.

PUTTING MORE TOOLS IN YOUR STRESS MANAGEMENT TOOLBOX

Looking at your coping skills inventory probably gives you a pretty clear idea of where you could strengthen your stress management skills. Let's walk through a few ideas for how you can build some new coping strategies.

🌀 STRESSFUL DAY SELF-CARE TOOLBOX

One of the first things we need to do when stressed is calm down. When we're stressed or upset it is difficult to think clearly or make a good plan for handling the situation. Using self-care and relaxation skills in times of stress helps us get calm enough to move forward in helpful ways.

Below are some common categories of self-care activities. Circle the ones that you'd enjoy or find relaxing, and add any others you know you like!

Self-Care Ideas

SOOTHING	EMOTIONAL
Hot bath	Journal how you're feeling
Meditation or deep breathing	Take yourself on an adventure
Yoga or stretching	Put on calming music
Burn a scented candle	Connect with a friend
Snuggle with your pet	Collect quotes

SELF-COMPASSION	EXPRESSIVE
Say a self-affirmation	Draw, paint, or do an art project
Make a gratitude list	Make a mood board
Get to bed on time	Cook or bake
Smile at yourself in the mirror	Sing or dance
Follow your hygiene routine	Say thank you

My Stressful Day Self-Care Plan

Write down three things you can do to take care of yourself on a stressful day.

1. _____

2. _____

3. _____

IDEA! Keep your list of self-care strategies in a note on your phone so you can access it anytime!

We can also think about self-care activities in terms of what they do for us—do they help us calm down our bodies, or do they help us reframe our thoughts? Let's look at some of the different things we can do for each purpose.

◎ GET CALM

Make sure your body is as calm as it can be. When your body is calm, you can make good decisions, solve problems, and act safely. Look at the ways to calm down listed here and circle the ones you think would work best for you:

Deep breathing

Take a walk

Listen to music

Journal

Stretching/yoga

Hot bath

◎ RETRAIN YOUR THOUGHTS

Check those negative, self-critical, or pessimistic thoughts that tend to sneak in on stressful days. When we find positive, encouraging, and kind thoughts, we feel better. Look at the encouraging, self-kindness thoughts below and circle the ones that resonate most with you:

I can handle this.

I trust things will get better.

I am strong and capable.

I'll figure it out.

It'll be okay.

I have strengths I can apply to this situation.

◎ ASK FOR HELP

When we're stressed, it can really help to reach out to our support system for advice, help, or simply words of encouragement.

◎ MY STRESSFUL DAY GO-TOS

When I'm feeling stressed, I can calm down by: _____

An encouraging thought I can use is: _____

I can ask this person for support: _____

MY SUPPORT CIRCLE

Being able to ask others for help when we're stressed is a great life skill, and one that can really improve your mood. Asking for help can mean lots of different things—from simply asking someone to hang out and distract us from our bad mood, all the way to telling someone what's going on and asking for help.

It is important to recognize that sometimes these are different people. The people you might enjoy spending time with just for fun may not be the same people you feel safe talking about your problems with. That's totally normal! It's good to have different kinds of support in our lives.

Let's look at who you can lean on for support:

⟳ MY SUPPORT CIRCLE – PEOPLE I ENJOY SPENDING TIME WITH

First let's write down all the people in your life that you simply enjoy spending time with. These are people you might choose to text or hang out with when you're feeling down or stressed.

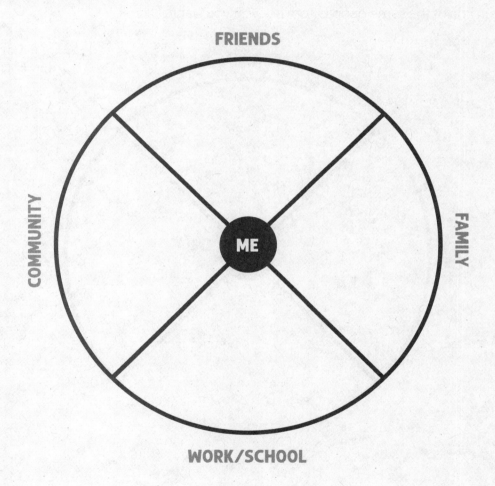

◎ MY SUPPORT CIRCLE – PEOPLE I CAN RELY ON FOR HELP

Next, let's write down a list of people you could lean on for help in hard times. These are people you might talk to about your problems, who you'd be comfortable sharing your feelings with, or who might be able to help you solve a problem. Yes, you can use some of the same people from above if you want!

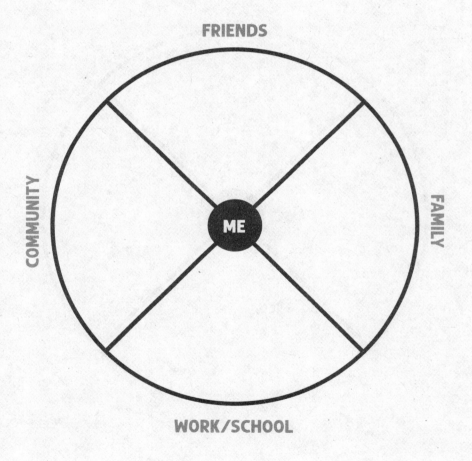

Building new coping skills takes time. Most of the rest of this workbook is dedicated to helping you build new, more helpful strategies for managing your mood and handling stress. Let's keep going!

CHAPTER 8

RETRAIN YOUR BRAIN

It's really easy to get in the habit of thinking negatively about ourselves and our life, especially when we're depressed. Negative thoughts are a big part of the downward spiral of depression—when stress happens, we blame ourselves and think everything sucks. That makes us feel even more down, and our depressed brain keeps sending us more and more negative thoughts to focus on.

Training your brain to catch those negative thoughts and change them to more positive ones interrupts that depression spiral. It's hard work, but worth it!

There are two steps to interrupting this depression spiral of negative mood and negative thinking. First, we have to recognize our own negative thinking patterns and learn how to replace negative depression thoughts with more realistic, positive, or helpful thoughts. Second, we need to start filling our mental bucket with helpful thoughts, so that we can keep that spiral from taking over.

Let's get started!

COMMON NEGATIVE THINKING PATTERNS

There are many ways our brain has of convincing us that things are bad—that the world is scary, that we are not good enough, or that the people around us don't care. Below are the most common negative thinking patterns that can cause and maintain depression. We often call these "thinking traps," or "cognitive distortions," because they trap your brain in a cycle of negative thoughts and feelings, even when those thoughts aren't accurate, fair, or helpful (Beck 1976).

Thinking Trap #1: Black-and-White Thinking

Do you ever think you have to be perfect or else? Do you find that you either love or hate most people or most things? Do you think that when you've failed, there's no point in trying again?

You might have fallen into the trap of black-or-white thinking. This thinking trap forces our brain into extremes, seeing everything—ourselves and others—as either all good or all bad. Perfectionism is a common problem with black-and-white thinking—we start to believe that anything less than perfect isn't worth doing. Being judgmental or easily offended by people can also be a sign of black-and-white thinking—finding yourself saying that someone is bad if they make a mistake, or that you hate them if they inadvertently upset you.

Black-and-white thinking can make depression worse because it tends to make us highly self-critical. It can also make it hard to tolerate small setbacks, as we evaluate them as huge failures. It can also interfere with healthy relationships, because when we box people into categories of good or bad, strong or weak, or love or hate, we make it hard to accept the inevitable ups and downs of human relationships or be understanding when those around us make mistakes.

The truth is, most things in life are neither perfectly black nor perfectly white. We all have strengths and weaknesses, make good and less-than-good decisions, and are works in progress. Learning to think more flexibly can really improve mood and well-being!

Write about a time you used black-and-white thinking.

Thinking Trap #2: It's All About Me

There are a lot of names for this thinking trap, including "personalization" and the very fancy phrase "self-referential thinking." But they all mean the same thing—a tendency to think everything that happens is specifically targeted at us personally. Running late for school and the traffic is backed up? The world is out to get you. Teacher hands out a pop quiz? She's trying to make you fail. You see a picture of some friends at the mall without you? They're purposely excluding you. The it's-all-about-me thinking trap tricks us into believing that other peoples' actions are targeted directly at us.

The other side of the it's-all-about-me coin is self-blame. Whatever goes wrong around us, we think—or worry—it's our fault. Parents are fighting? It's because of me. My best friend is upset? I probably did something wrong. Someone didn't say hi to me in the hall? They don't like me anymore.

This thinking trap puts us in the center of every story. While some amount of self-focus is normal and appropriate—we do want to know how we impact our world and how our world impacts us—always interpreting events through this thinking trap causes unnecessary self-blame and can cause us to feel more rejected, hurt, or excluded than others ever intended. As a result, this thinking trap can keep us stuck in a depression spiral of negative thoughts and feelings.

Learning to put events in perspective is a great life skill that can foster more positive thinking. Later in this chapter, we'll work on learning to see things from multiple points of view.

REFLECTION *Write about a time you saw a situation only from your own point of view.*

REFLECTION

_____

_____

_____

_____

Thinking Trap #3: Crystal Ball

Imagine you're getting ready for high school soccer tryouts. You played some soccer in middle school but maybe not at a very competitive level. Your friend invites you to a drop-in skills practice to tune up a bit before tryouts next month. You think on it but decide not to go because *I won't make a high school team anyway.*

Uh-oh! You've fallen for the crystal ball thinking trap. This is when your brain decides it is a fortune teller, able to predict the future AND read other peoples' minds! It would be amazing if that were true...but since it isn't, this thinking trap often leads us to make mistakes.

A teacher walks by you and doesn't say hi: *He totally doesn't like me.*

Your mom texts that she wants to talk to you about something: *I'm in trouble.*

A classmate looks your way during class: *She thinks I'm a total weirdo.*

These are all great examples of our brain tricking us into thinking we know what other people are thinking and what is going to happen in the future, even when we don't have any data to support our conclusions. And when the crystal ball thinking trap collides with the it's-all-about-me tendency to self-blame and the black-and-white thinking tendency to think the worst...we get some pretty negative thoughts.

Learning to slow our brains down and look at all possible outcomes is a great way to get out of this thinking trap.

REFLECTION

Write about a time you thought you knew what someone was thinking, but it didn't turn out that way.

Thinking Trap #4: Gray-Colored Glasses

Have you heard of rose-colored glasses? They're from a saying about people who are super optimistic, always see the best in a situation, and expect good things to happen—we say they see life through "rose-colored glasses."

Well...people with depression have their own set of glasses. Except depression glasses aren't tinted in rose or gold, and they're not even simply clear. Depression glasses are colored gray.

The gray-colored glasses thinking trap tricks us into seeing everything through dull, depression-tinted lenses. We look at any situation and immediately zoom in on the negative features, and we discount or ignore any positive features. This thinking trap is like a filter—it is like our gray-colored glasses filter out all the good so we only see the bad.

At the team social dinner, you only notice who doesn't speak to you...but not who does.

After a math quiz, you hyperfocus on the problems you got wrong...but don't think about the ones you got right.

When looking at yourself in the mirror, you only see the slightly crooked nose...but not your bright eyes or long hair.

You sit down to dinner, and all you can think about is all the homework you have... but not that your mom made your favorite foods.

This is looking at the world through gray-colored glasses.

Most situations—and most people!—have both positive and negative features. We can choose which to focus on. Taking off those gray-colored glasses can help us see the world in a more balanced *and* more positive light.

Write about a time you focused on the negatives in a situation.

_____

_____

_____

_____

_____

Thinking Trap #5: Emotion Brain

Have you ever seen a little kid on a playground get really upset when he falls down after a kid bumps into him? The kid feels hurt, angry, maybe even embarrassed to have fallen down. That kid might immediately start yelling, "You pushed me!" to the kid who bumped into him.

This is a great example of emotion brain. The kid feels angry and hurt, so he's sure he was wronged in some way. But actually...it was just an accident.

I'm really anxious about going to practice today—it'll be hard and I'll do terribly.

I don't feel like going to my cousin's party—it won't be any fun.

I'm overwhelmed thinking about all my math homework—it's too much to even try to do.

Have you ever had thoughts like this? You find yourself feeling really bad—anxious, down, or overwhelmed—and that makes it hard to find the energy, motivation, or desire to do things you used to do?

You might have fallen into the emotion brain thinking trap.

Emotion brain is when we make interpretations about ourselves, others, or situations based on how we feel. The problem isn't our feelings—feelings are valid—but that those feelings may reflect our underlying anxiety, depression, or low self-esteem, rather than what's actually happening in our lives. Letting our emotions rule our thoughts keeps that depression spiral spinning us down.

One of the worst emotion brain loops is when we feel bad about ourselves, and start to think that must be true.

I feel unlovable, so I must be unloved.

I feel worthless, so I must be worthless.

I feel like a bad person, so I must be a bad person.

See how that works? Since depression often makes us feel really down, lonely, and bad about ourselves, if we think those feelings are what is really true, we can get sucked down into the spiral.

Challenging emotion brain means being willing to say that how you feel may not be what is really happening.

REFLECTION *Write about a time you felt something and thought it must be true.*

REFLECTION

_____

_____

_____

_____

BREAKING OUT OF THINKING TRAPS

The first step to breaking out of these depression thinking traps is to realize you're stuck in one. Our thoughts often feel real and true, so this can be harder than it seems. A couple of tips:

Look for Strong Emotions

When you have a strong emotional response to something, especially a strong negative emotion, that might be a good time to try to catch the thought that goes along with it.

EXAMPLE: I feel really down this afternoon.

THOUGHT CHECK: "I'll never get all my homework done."

"My friends ignored me at school today."

When we can point a finger to the thoughts that go along with our big emotions, we often find those thinking traps.

"I'll never get all my homework done." → Sounds like the crystal ball! Predicting the future and assuming it will be bad.

"My friends ignored me at school today." → Could be some "it's all about me" going on, assuming that if someone didn't speak to you, it was an intentional insult.

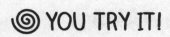 YOU TRY IT!

Write down a time today you had a strong emotion:

_____

_____

_____

What were you thinking?

_____

_____

_____

Do you think you fell into any thinking traps? (Hint: sometimes we fall into more than one thinking trap at the same time. If you're not sure which one you got caught in, circle all that might apply.)

Black-and-white thinking

It's all about me

Crystal ball

Gray-colored glasses

Emotion brain

Look for Stressful Events

When something happens that is unusual or stressful, our brain often rushes to fill in the blanks with interpretation. That can be a great opportunity to catch those negative thoughts.

EXAMPLE: There was a pop quiz in history class today.

THOUGHT CHECK: "I'm never prepared for these things."

"It was a terrible day at school."

When we can figure out how we react to events, we can get better at finding our thoughts.

"I'm never prepared for these things." → Sounds like black-and-white thinking! Seeing this quiz in all-or-nothing terms—like "never" being prepared.

"It was a terrible day at school." → Could be gray-colored glasses? Evaluating the whole day through the one negative event that happened.

◎ YOU TRY IT!

Write down something that happened today:

_____

_____

_____

What were you thinking?

_____

_____

_____

Do you think you fell into any thinking traps? (Hint: sometimes we fall into more than one thinking trap. If you're not sure which one, circle all that might apply.)

> Black-and-white thinking
>
> It's all about me
>
> Crystal ball
>
> Gray-colored glasses
>
> Emotion brain

REFRAMING NEGATIVE THOUGHTS

Just like depression can train our brain to think negative and unhelpful thoughts, we can retrain our brain to think positive and helpful ones instead. Like any new skill, it just takes practice. This is called "reframing"—when we take a negative thought and try to think about it in a different way.

The best way to practice reframing is to (1) catch the negative thought and then (2) ask yourself: Can I think about this another way?

For example, let's imagine that you didn't make the team you tried out for and that many of your friends are on. You might think things such as:

"They won't want to be friends with me anymore."

"I'm not good enough."

Reframing doesn't try to pretend the situation isn't stressful or hard. Rather, reframing tries to see if there's any more balanced, realistic, or hopeful way to look at the hard situation. In this case, some possible reframes might be:

"We can do things outside of team events to stay friends."

"I'm disappointed and wish I'd done better, but it doesn't mean I'm not a good person."

Below are some examples of how you might take a negative thought and try to reframe it.

REFRAMING NEGATIVE THOUGHTS

INSTEAD OF...	TRY...
I suck.	I'm still learning and improving.
It's all my fault.	I can take responsibility for my part but not blame myself.
The world is so unfair.	The world can be both hard and amazing.
It'll never get better.	It's hard to see now, but I trust things will get better.
I'm a horrible person.	I'm not perfect, but I do my best.
Everyone hates me.	I have people who love and accept me for who I am.
I ruined everything.	I made a mistake, but I can do my best to fix it.
Everything sucks.	Things are hard right now, but I trust they'll get better.

Let's practice!

Below are some examples of the negative thoughts from this chapter and some more balanced, realistic, and helpful thoughts. See if you can try reframing the rest!

REFRAMING NEGATIVE THOUGHTS: SELF-PRACTICE

SITUATION	OLD NEGATIVE THOUGHT	REFRAMING: NEW HELPFUL THOUGHT
Running late for school and traffic is bad.	The world is out to get me.	Not the best day for traffic, but it's so hard to predict.
Teacher walks by you and doesn't say hi.	He hates me.	He's so busy, he probably didn't even see me.
Mom texts she wants to talk to you.	I'm in trouble.	I wonder what's up?
Math quiz is returned.	Look at all the problems I got wrong.	I got many problems right, but there are a few I didn't know.
Soccer practice after school.	I'm going to mess up.	I'm still working on mastering those new drills.
Family birthday party.	I won't have any fun.	It's only a few hours, and I can get through it.
Lot of homework.	I'm so overwhelmed—I'll never get it all done.	
Dinnertime.	I don't have time to sit and eat.	
Team social event.	No one likes me.	
See a photo on social media.	My friends are having fun and didn't include me.	

Not sure if a thought is negative or helpful? Ask yourself: Does this thought make me feel better or help me do better? If the answer is no, try finding a more helpful thought.

⊚ YOU TRY IT!

First, pick a recent situation that was stressful or upsetting.

SITUATION:

Next, write down two to three negative or self-blaming thoughts you had about it.

IDENTIFYING NEGATIVE THOUGHTS

1	Thought:
2	Thought:
3	Thought:

Now, try to find another way to think about the situation. Can you reframe each thought to a more helpful one?

IDENTIFYING AND CHANGING NEGATIVE THOUGHTS

1	Thought:	New thought:
2	Thought:	New thought:
3	Thought:	New thought:

Finally, here are some more general helpful thoughts to consider when you're feeling stuck or down. They're also useful things to remind yourself when you feel a thinking trap creeping up on you.

POSITIVE REMINDERS

I'm doing the best I can.	I'm a good person.	I can do this.	Everyone struggles sometimes.
I'm learning and growing.	I have strengths I can apply to this situation.	It'll be okay.	I can handle this.
I have a lot to look forward to.	I'll figure it out.	I deserve good things.	I see the good in me.

Great work!

Retraining your brain takes time. As often as you can, try to catch your thinking traps and reframe them into more helpful thoughts!

PART 3

IMPROVE MOTIVATION

One of the sneakiest things about downward depression spirals is how they impact your motivation. When you feel down and low energy, it's natural to not want to do anything. When you're not feeling motivated, it's easy to fall behind on things you need to do, such as homework, chores, or even self-care.

But when you're a teen, falling behind on homework or other responsibilities often has consequences. Your grades suffer, your parents or teachers may get frustrated with you, and you might not be able to meet your personal goals. And when we feel like we're letting others down—or letting ourselves down—we feel even worse...that's the depression spiral at work.

Improving motivation is a key part of breaking out of the depression spiral. The last several chapters helped you feel better. These next three chapters will help you build up your ability to get and stay motivated, so that you can get things done and rebuild your life.

84

CHAPTER 9

NO MORE PROCRASTINATION BRAIN

Do you find it hard to motivate yourself to do the things you know you need to do? Have you fallen behind on your schoolwork? Are you struggling to get your chores done?

If so, you're not alone. Depression can make it difficult to feel motivated or maintain focus. It's hard to care about things like school, chores, or other tasks when you feel so down, and even if you want to get things done, you might find that you have little energy, motivation, or ability to focus when you try.

 **REFLECTION** *How has depression affected your motivation?*

Most teens struggle to maintain focus from time to time, and depression can make it even harder. When we're feeling down, unmotivated, and tired, it can be difficult to concentrate. You might find that your mind is wandering to negative thoughts or feelings or things you're stressed about. You might find that you feel overwhelmed by all that you need to do and can't focus on what's right in front of you. You might find that you keep putting things off until they pile up and you feel totally overwhelmed.

REFLECTION
REFLECTION *How has your focus and concentration been lately?*

Luckily, whichever of these issues you struggle with, these next three chapters are here to help! Using tips and strategies from current neuroscience research, we'll work on breaking down procrastination thoughts, setting goals, and improving focus. These strategies will help you be more productive and get things done—and as it turns out, when we get done what needs to get done, we feel better about ourselves!

PROCRASTINATION BRAIN

One of the biggest challenges to focus is procrastination. When we feel over-whelmed, we tend to cope by procrastinating. We put off what feels too difficult to do. The problem is that the more we procrastinate, the bigger and bigger the task seems to get. We then feel even more overwhelmed, and it's even harder to get started. Sound familiar? Yep! Turns out that procrastination is one of the downward spirals of depression.

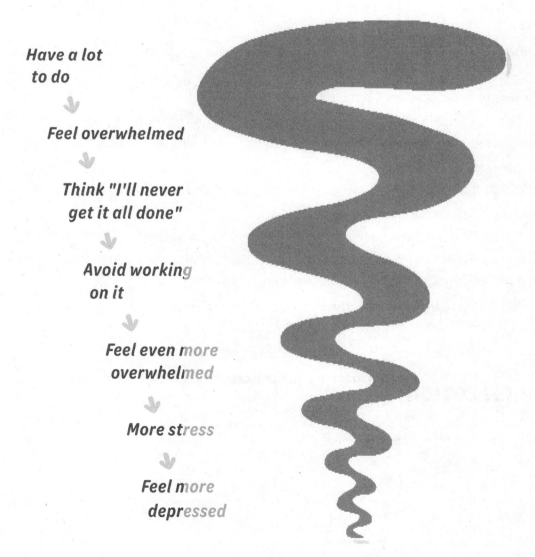

*Have a lot
to do*

Feel overwhelmed

*Think "I'll never
get it all done"*

*Avoid working
on it*

*Feel even more
overwhelmed*

More stress

*Feel more
depressed*

REFLECTION

Does this describe you at all? Is procrastination a problem for you?

_____

_____

_____

When we have a big project, a lot of homework, a big test to study for, or another major task in front of us, it is easy to feel overwhelmed. We might start to think, "I'll never get it all done" or "It's too much to handle."

This is procrastination brain! You've probably fallen into one of the thinking traps we talked about in chapter 8. The two most common thinking traps that cause procrastination are crystal ball and emotion brain.

Crystal ball makes us believe we know the future. We start to think thoughts like, "I'll never get it done" or "I'll probably fail anyway."

Emotion brain makes us think that how we feel about our big project is what is real. We feel overwhelmed, so we think the project actually is overwhelming. We start to think thoughts like, "I can't do this" or "It's too much."

And before we know it, procrastination brain has taken over!

REFLECTION

What are your procrastination brain thinking traps?

_____

_____

_____

Luckily, we learned in chapter 8 how to recognize these thinking traps and break out of them. So let's try it!

◎ PINNING DOWN THE PROCRASTINATION THOUGHTS

Think about a recent project or situation in which you procrastinated.

Situation:

Next, write down two to three procrastination brain thoughts you had about that situation that kept you procrastinating.

IDENTIFYING PROCRASTINATION THOUGHTS

1	Thought:
2	Thought:
3	Thought:

Now, try to find another way to think about the situation. Can you reframe each procrastination thought to a more helpful one?

IDENTIFYING AND CHANGING PROCRASTINATION THOUGHTS

E X A M P L E	Thought: I'll never get it all done.	New thought: It's a lot to do, but I've gotten big projects done before.
1	Thought:	New thought:
2	Thought:	New thought:
3	Thought:	New thought:

Thinking more helpful thoughts can make you feel less overwhelmed. And that's the first step in building motivation. In addition to thinking more positively, there are specific strategies you can use to get things done. In the next chapter, we'll work on how to use goal setting to break a big task into smaller, more manageable tasks, so that you don't feel so overwhelmed. After that, we'll also work on how to stay focused during your work times.

CHAPTER 10

SET GOALS

How do you eat an elephant?

ONE BITE AT A TIME

WHAT IS A SMART GOAL?

It's a super useful tool in fighting procrastination and depression. In fact, the first step to getting things done is to set SMART goals. SMART goals take the giant elephant and turn it into bite-size pieces (Doran 1981).

SMART goals are:

- **SPECIFIC**
- **MEASURABLE**
- **ACHIEVABLE**
- **RELEVANT**
- **TIME-BOUND**

LET'S LOOK AT EACH PART OF A SMART GOAL.

SPECIFIC

A specific goal is one that is well defined, clear, and easy to understand, with actionable steps.

Example of a nonspecific goal: I will study harder.

Example of a specific goal: I will work on my math grade by going to office hours to ask for help on this chapter.

MEASURABLE

You can only know if you've achieved your goal if you know how to measure success. Make sure you know when you've made it!

Example of an unmeasurable goal: I'll get more exercise.

Example of a measurable goal: I'll do ten minutes of exercise four times this week.

ACHIEVABLE

This is another way of saying *realistic*. If you're currently failing three subjects and there's only three weeks left in the term, it may not be realistic to say "I'll get straight As this semester." Achievable goals help you see what the next step is from where you're starting.

Example of an unachievable goal: I'll run a marathon this month.

Example of an achievable goal: I'll double my run distance this month from two miles to four miles.

RELEVANT

Relevant goals are ones that matter—they impact areas of your life that you put value on. Being able to fit twenty-five pieces of gum in your mouth at once might be a fun goal, but it isn't likely to be a relevant goal that helps you achieve what you want to achieve or get done the things that need to get done.

Example of an irrelevant goal: I'm going to watch all *The Lord of the Rings* movies in one sitting.

Example of a relevant goal: I'm going to invite my friend Jordan over on Sunday to watch the movie we were assigned for English class.

TIME-BOUND

Goals work best if you know exactly when you should have achieved them by or how long you should work at them for. Time-bound goals help us manage our attention and focus on what is reasonable. It is best to have short-term goals (within a day or week) and goals that require smaller spurts of energy (an hour or two at most).

Example of a non-time-bound goal: I'm going to work on my Spanish project today.

Example of a time-bound goal: After school, I'm going to spend thirty minutes outlining the project content, and then thirty minutes creating the first five slides.

REFLECTION

REFLECTION

Have you ever set a goal that you ended up not meeting? What happened?

_____

_____

_____

LET'S PRACTICE!

Remember Sam, from chapter 1? He moved to a new town and is really struggling to find any motivation to do schoolwork. His parents are on his case to get his grades back up. Sam wants to do better in school, but he's so behind and doesn't know where to start. Let's help Sam set a SMART goal to improve his grades.

Sam tries to set a goal: I'm going to get my grades up! My goal is to get back to all As and Bs.

Sounds good, right? He wants to try to improve his grades, and is setting what seems like a clear goal: all As and Bs. But let's look deeply at how SMART this goal is.

Sam's goal: Get my grades up to all As and Bs.

SPECIFIC? Sort of. It isn't super general like, "I want to do better," but it also isn't clear which classes he'll focus on.

MEASURABLE? Again, kind of. Whether his grades end up As or Bs will be measurable...at some point. It would be better if Sam knew when to evaluate his progress. At the end of the month? End of the semester? End of the year?

ACHIEVABLE? It's hard to know without knowing where Sam is starting. If he currently has mostly As and Bs with, let's say, one C in history, this seems achievable. But if he has Cs or below in multiple classes, this might be a difficult goal to reach.

RELEVANT? Definitely. He takes pride in being a good student, this is an area he values, and it sounds like it is one his parents are pushing him on as well.

TIME-BOUND? Hmmm...not quite yet.

Let's help Sam try again!

Sam's new goal: I'm going to get my history grade from a C to a B by the end of this semester.

SPECIFIC? Better! We know the subject, the desired result, and the timeline—though we don't really know *what* Sam is going to do or *how* he will improve his grade.

MEASURABLE? Yes, we will know if his grade is a B clearly at the end of the semester.

ACHIEVABLE? Maybe. It doesn't sound unrealistic, but we also don't know where Sam is struggling in history—does he have a C because he isn't turning assignments in, because he keeps doing poorly on exams, or because he isn't understanding the material when he writes essays?

RELEVANT? Definitely. He takes pride in being a good student, this is an area he values, and it sounds like it is one his parents are pushing him on as well.

TIME-BOUND? Better—by the end of the semester is time-bound. But it is also quite a ways away, and it can be hard to sustain motivation for multiple weeks. It would be better if Sam focused on what he could do today or this week to improve his history grade.

Let's help Sam get to a great SMART goal!

SAM'S NEW GOAL: This week, I'm going to work on my history grade by doing the worksheet on the in-class movie on Tuesday night, turning it in on Wednesday, and going to office hours on Thursday to ask the teacher for help understanding the essay assignment.

SPECIFIC? Yes! We know what subject, what timeline, and what specific actions Sam plans to take.

MEASURABLE? Yes! Sam will know by Thursday if he did these three things: the worksheet, turning it in, and talking to his teacher.

ACHIEVABLE? It's a little hard to be sure because we don't know exactly where Sam is in terms of homework and energy for school, but it's three relatively small, clear actions (worksheet, turning it in, talking to a teacher), and he thinks it is achievable, so let's give it a try!

RELEVANT? Yes, this continues to be a relevant goal for Sam!

TIME-BOUND? Yes! This newly framed goal is very clear on what Sam needs to do each day this week to achieve his goal.

WHAT'S RELEVANT TO YOU?

The best way to start making goals is to identify one or two areas of your life you'd like to improve in. These can be achievement goals (school, grades, sports); personal self-care goals (exercise, hygiene, sleep, relaxation); social goals (friendships, social activity); family goals (communication with parents); extracurricular goals (clubs, sports, hobbies); or any other goals that have meaning to you!

REFLECTION
REFLECTION
What do you want to work on?

Now let's pick one of them to work on. What's something relevant to you that you would like to set a goal toward?

Let's break it down! Set two SMART goals that you can work on this week to help you make progress in this area.

EXAMPLE: Jesse wants to spend less time on social media because she finds it makes her feel worse about herself. She currently comes home from school and spends up to three hours just scrolling TikTok and Instagram before doing anything else.

Great overall goal! Two SMART goals this week might be:

SMART GOAL #1: On Monday when I get home from school, I will set a timer for fifteen minutes. I can be on my phone for fifteen minutes, and then when the timer goes off, I will start my homework. I will do my homework for sixty minutes, then let myself have another fifteen minutes of social media.

SMART GOAL #2: I will invite a friend to do homework with me on Wednesday after school. While I'm with my friend, I will not look at social media.

Great job, Jesse! These are two very specific, measurable, achievable, relevant, and time-bound goals for this week. They don't magically solve the big issue of too much time on social media and feeling bad about herself, but they are clear steps toward something that's important to her to improve on.

⌾ YOU TRY IT!

Look back at what you wrote for what is relevant to you. Use that to set an overall goal for something you want to work on.

MY OVERALL GOAL:

_____

_____

_____

Now set two SMART goals that will help you achieve this:

SMART GOAL #1:

_____

_____

SMART GOAL #2:

_____

_____

Great work! Being able to set SMART goals is the first step to motivating yourself to becoming the person you want to be and build the life you want to live.

⊚ SET A SMART GOAL

Free tool available: http://www.newharbinger.com/53479

My goal: _____

SPECIFIC	*What exactly do I need to do to achieve this goal?*	
MEASURABLE	*How will I know if I have achieved my goal?*	
ACHIEVABLE	*Is this a realistic goal? What steps do I need to take to make it realistic?*	
RELEVANT	*Why is this goal important to me?*	
TIME-BOUND	*What is my deadline for this goal? Can I achieve it this week?*	

CHAPTER 11

BUILD FOCUS

Focus can be a big problem in getting things done and meeting personal goals. Many things impact focus, including being tired, having too much to do, and distractions such as social media. Your mood can also impact your focus—when you feel down or anxious it can be hard to concentrate.

But there are ways to increase your ability to focus and get things done. This chapter will introduce simple strategies to break big projects down into smaller, more manageable tasks, so that you don't feel so overwhelmed. We'll also work on how to stay focused during your work times.

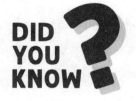 Neuroscience research shows that people can only concentrate on one thing for about ten to fifteen minutes at a time (Bradbury 2016).

IDENTIFY YOUR FOCUS BUSTERS

First things first! We can't focus hard on a project every minute of every day. The brain needs time to wake up, to calm down, and to get in the right frame of mind to focus. The first thing you need to do is set yourself up for success.

What gets in the way of focusing for you? Below are the most common challenges to focusing.

DISTRACTIONS: If the human brain is not very good at focusing on one thing, it is truly terrible at trying to do many things at once. Checking social media, texting friends, and having videos playing in the background can all be distractions that make it difficult to focus.

LACK OF PURPOSE: It can be hard to focus when we are not sure what we're doing or why it matters. For example, "reading something" is very different from "reading something so that you can answer the three questions at the end of the chapter." Knowing the purpose of what we're trying to do can help motivate us to focus.

ENVIRONMENT: Most of us do better at focusing when things around us are calm and quiet. Trying to focus in busy places with lots of people is likely to be more difficult than trying to focus alone in a quiet room.

PHYSICAL NEEDS: If we're hungry, tired, or really upset it can be hard to get the mind to focus on anything else. Most of us also have natural biorhythms that impact focus—there are times of the day when we're naturally sharper and other times when we're naturally lower energy.

REFLECTION
REFLECTION

What helps you focus? What do you find gets in the way?

DID YOU KNOW?

The afternoon "slump" is a real thing! For most people, the late afternoon (3 to 5 p.m.) is a natural low-energy point (Suni 2023). Our circadian rhythms have natural alert and drowsy times. Every body is different, though.

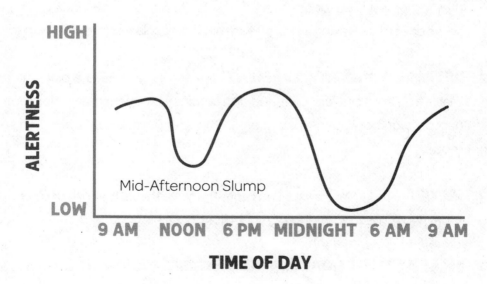

REFLECTION
REFLECTION *When is it easiest for you to focus? When is it hardest?*

_____

_____

_____

PLAN FOR PRODUCTIVITY

There are things you can do to set yourself up for success when you need to focus and get work done. Here are a few of the key points:

1. **PREPARE YOURSELF:** As we talked about, no one focuses well when they're hungry, tired, or stressed. Consider having a small snack to give you some energy and taking ten to fifteen minutes to relax before you try to focus.

2. **PREPARE YOUR ENVIRONMENT:** Make sure you have a place to work that is free from clutter, noise, and distractions. Have your materials prepared (laptop, workbook, pens, paper, etc.). Consider putting your phone on silent mode.

3. **MAKE A LIST:** Make a list of no more than five things that need to get done today. No more than five! Be as specific as possible.

4. **MAKE A SMART GOAL FOR YOUR WORK SESSION:** For example, rather than saying, "I'm going to work on homework," say, "I'm going to do the first ten problems in my math assignment." We'll talk in a minute about "chunking" work into small pieces.

Below are some common barriers to focusing with some possible solutions. You may have others you want to add to the blank rows below!

BUSTING FOCUS BUSTERS

WHAT MAKES IT HARD TO FOCUS	HOW TO SOLVE THE PROBLEM
Being tired after a long day at school.	Take a break before you try to focus.
I feel disorganized—I don't have what I need to do my work.	Spend time preparing for your work session by gathering materials and making a plan.
I don't know what I'm supposed to do.	Ask a peer, parent, teacher, or coach for clarification on the assignment.
I feel overwhelmed by how much I have to do.	Take some deep breaths and make one SMART goal for the next hour only.
I'm stressed about something going on in my life.	Take some deep breaths and try to redirect attention to the work in front of you. Set smaller SMART goals when you're stressed.
I just don't care right now.	Consider writing yourself a reminder note about why you want to achieve your goals as motivation for these times. Refer to it as often as you need to!

WHAT MAKES IT HARD TO FOCUS	HOW TO SOLVE THE PROBLEM

ONE BITE AT A TIME: HOW CHUNKING HELPS US FOCUS

Remember how we eat an elephant? One bite at a time! Chunking is a time-management strategy that helps us break off bite-size pieces of whatever it is we need to get done.

What Is Chunking?

Chunking is a way of blocking time so that you have a short chunk of work time, a break, and then another short chunk of work, and so on. Chunking can look like this:

15 minutes work

5 minutes break

15 minutes work

5 minutes break

After you've done four rounds of working, treat yourself to a fifteen-minute break!

How Does Chunking Work?

Remember that statistic we saw earlier, that people can only concentrate on one thing for ten to fifteen minutes at a time? Chunking helps us use our brain efficiently. We focus for short bursts, then give our brain a break.

But...I Can't Take a Break if I Haven't Gotten Everything Done Yet!

Ah...! This is the heart of the dilemma of productivity. We often believe we don't "deserve" a break until we get everything done. But the truth is that if we try too hard to focus when our brain is maxed out, we aren't productive anyway. Even worse, we get really frustrated with ourselves for not getting work done. It's another bad downward spiral!

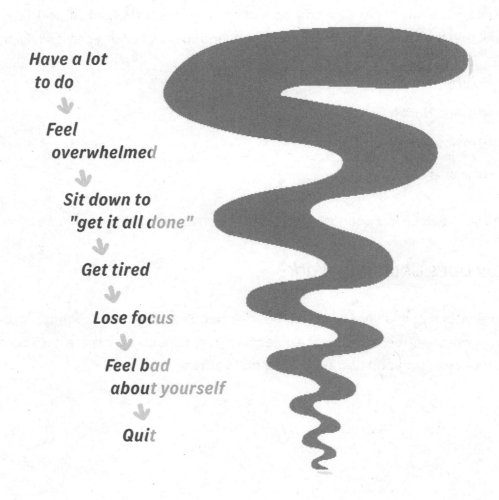

Have a lot
to do

Feel
overwhelmed

Sit down to
"get it all done"

Get tired

Lose focus

Feel bad
about yourself

Quit

Chunking helps us reverse that downward spiral!

Have a *lot to do*

⬇

Chunk time

⬇

Have a SMART goal for each chunk

⬇

Work for fifteen minutes

⬇

Take a break

⬇

Stay focused

⬇

Get things done!

Chunking + SMART Goals for the Win!

We can combine these two strategies to make a productivity plan for times you need to get work done.

Let's imagine that you have three hours to get your homework done after school. You have a lot to do—a math problem set, an essay outline, some history chapter notes. You've just gotten home from school and are tired, hungry, and super not motivated to do any of it.

◎ SET YOURSELF UP FOR SUCCESS

PREPARE YOURSELF: Take fifteen minutes to get a snack and do some deep breathing or something relaxing.

REFLECTION: What else helps you relax and get ready to focus?

_____

_____

PREPARE YOUR ENVIRONMENT: Make sure you have a place to work that is free from clutter, noise, and distractions. Have your materials prepared (laptop, workbook, pens, paper, etc.). Consider putting your phone on silent mode.

REFLECTION: Where do you work best? What materials do you need for a homework session?

_____

_____

MAKE A LIST: Make a list of no more than five items that need to get done today. No more than five! Be as specific as possible.

My Five-Item To-Do List:

1. _____

_____

2. _____

_____

3. _____

_____

4. _____

_____

5. _____

_____

MAKE SMART GOALS FOR YOUR WORK SESSION: For example, rather than saying, "I'm going to work on homework," say, "I'm going to do the first ten problems in my math assignment."

Make a SMART goal for each item on your to-do list:

SMART GOAL #1: _____

_____

_____

SMART GOAL #2: _____

_____

_____

SMART GOAL #3: _____

_____

_____

SMART GOAL #4: _____

_____

_____

SMART GOAL #5: _____

_____

_____

CHUNK TIME: Work for fifteen minutes on SMART goal #1, then take a five-minute break. Repeat for four cycles, then take a fifteen-minute break.

REFLECTION

What can you do during your break? Ideas include stretching, grabbing a piece of candy or gum, and getting a glass of water. Something that moves your body is especially good. And avoid getting sucked into your phone!

_____

_____

_____

_____

_____

These strategies—SMART goals, preparing for productivity, and chunking time—can help us focus and get things done. And the more effective and productive we are, the better we feel. You got this!

◉ MY DAY PLANNER

Free tool available: http://www.newharbinger.com/53479

My #1 goal for the day is to: _____

PREPARE YOURSELF: Are you hungry, thirsty, comfortable?

PREPARE YOUR ENVIRONMENT: Do you have the materials you need? Are you in a place you can focus?

PLAN YOUR TIME: What do you plan to get done today?

TO DO!

Must-Do Tasks

1. _____

2. _____

3. _____

4. _____

5. _____

Can-Wait Tasks

1. _____

2. _____

3. _____

4. _____

5. _____

STAY FOCUSED!

Distractions

1. _____

2. _____

3. _____

4. _____

5. _____

How to Avoid Them

1. _____

2. _____

3. _____

4. _____

5. _____

SMART Goals

REMEMBER: Specific, Measurable, Achievable, Relevant, and Time-bound!

SMART GOAL #1: _____

_____

SMART GOAL #2: _____

_____

SMART GOAL #3: _____

_____

IDEA! POMODORO TECHNIQUE: Work for fifteen minutes then take a break for five minutes. Use the timer on your phone to keep on track.

PART 4

BUILD THE LIFE YOU WANT TO LIVE

Sometimes it feels like everyone is telling you what *not* to do. Stop procrastinating. Stop isolating. Stop being so negative.

And sometimes, it is true that our depression downward spiral has sucked us into some unhelpful thoughts and behaviors that need to be undone. In the last sections, you worked on how to undo some of the thoughts and behaviors that cause depression, and how to replace them with more helpful thoughts and behaviors.

But that's not the only way to reverse the downward spiral of depression. Positive psychology is a way of looking at mental health through a different lens (Seligman and Csikszentmihalyi 2000). Rather than identifying all the unhelpful things we need to *stop doing*, positive psychology helps us identify all the things we should *start doing* and *keep doing*. Positive psychology helps us recognize our own strengths and use them to build the life we want to live. We each have strengths and values that make us unique, special individuals. Leaning into these strengths and values is a great way to turn that downward spiral of depression into an upward one!

In this section, we will look at how you can build the life you want to live. Depression can cause poor self-esteem, social isolation, and difficulties seeing the world in a positive light. In the next four chapters, we'll challenge those tendencies by learning to identify and invest in strengths, build gratitude and positive thinking, and develop stronger social connections. Let's get started!

CHAPTER 12

WHO AM I? IDENTIFYING STRENGTHS

Personal strengths are aspects of our personality and identity that make us unique. Strengths don't have to be associated with objective achievements—for example, love of learning can be a personal strength even if you sometimes struggle to get the grades you want in class. Grades are an aspect of performance, but strengths are the personal qualities that make you *you*. Leaning into strengths means using these as guiding principles to set goals, make choices, and guide behavior.

People who can identify their personal strengths and find ways to use them in their life tend to have higher self-esteem, find it easier to set and achieve goals, and are happier overall (Duan 2016).

The first step is to identify your personal strengths. Many of our best qualities go ignored because we don't recognize them as unique strengths—so getting clear on what our strengths are is the first step in learning to use them to our advantage.

Let's spend some time identifying your personal strengths. Below are some questions that can help you remember the special things about you that make you...you!

⊚ FIGURE OUT YOUR STRENGTHS

Reflection:

What kind of friend am I? How do I show support for the people in my life?

_____

_____

_____

_____

What do I love to do? What are some interests, hobbies, or activities that make me unique and set me apart from other kids?

_____

_____

_____

_____

Think about a recent time you felt confident. What were you doing?

_____

_____

_____

_____

Think about a recent time you felt happy. What were you doing?

_____

_____

_____

_____

Think about someone in your life who you admire. What do you admire about them?

_____

_____

_____

_____

⊚ SELF-DISCOVERY: IDENTIFYING YOUR PERSONAL STRENGTHS

Below is a list of many personal qualities (Park and Peterson 2006). Some might describe you and others might not. Start by circling *about ten* of these words that you believe describe you. Don't overthink it—you'll have the opportunity to narrow them down later. For now, circle all the words that you believe describe you.

FIND YOUR STRENGTHS

Creative	Independent	Strong	Curious	Kind
Helpful	Artistic	Wise	Mature	Competent
Friendly	Fair	Brave	Cooperative	Humble
Responsible	Confident	Energetic	Disciplined	Patient
Have good common sense	Funny	Love to learn	Grateful	Intelligent
Spiritual	Athletic	Assertive	Optimistic	Adventurous
Flexible	Enthusiastic	Honest	Open-minded	Persistent
Cheerful	Empathetic	Ambitious	Organized	Generous

Now, look at all the words you circled. Narrow it down to your top five strengths.

My Top Five Strengths

1. I am... _____

2. I am... _____

3. I am... _____

4. I am... _____

5. I am... _____

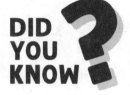 **DID YOU KNOW?** There are over half a million different combinations of five strengths from this list! People are so unique!

REFLECTION *Was this a hard activity for you? Did any of your personal strengths surprise you?*

_____

_____

_____

IDEA! A "strengths board" can be a motivating and fun way to remember your strengths. Fill a small posterboard with pictures or words that capture your personal strengths!

Many people find that they are a little surprised at the strengths they identify. It is easy to see ourselves in black-and-white terms—*I'm smart, but not creative; I'm kind, but not a good student; I'm passionate, but not disciplined*. Often, when we consider our whole self, we are able to see strengths we other times overlook!

CHAPTER 13

BUILD STRENGTHS

Now that you have identified your personal strengths, let's dig deeper into how you can apply them in your life. Strengths can guide how we show up in relationships, how we pursue and achieve our goals, and how we develop as a person. In this chapter, we're going to look at each strength you identified and examine how it *already shows up* in your life, as well as *new ways you can use that strength* to enhance your life.

There are many areas of our life where our strengths can show up and have a positive impact. Here are the most common:

 RELATIONSHIPS: How we interact with other people.

 ACHIEVEMENT: How we set and meet goals at school, work, sports, or other performance domains.

 PERSONAL GROWTH: How we develop hobbies, interests, and passions on our own.

The same strength might show up in one, two, or even all three areas of your life. For example, if one of your strengths is being enthusiastic, it might show up as:

RELATIONSHIPS: You're the friend whose enthusiasm brings the positive energy for trying new activities.

ACHIEVEMENT: Your enthusiasm might make you the loudest member of the cheer squad for your sports team.

PERSONAL GROWTH: You might be the kind of person who gets really excited to try new things.

See how that can work?

The important thing about strengths is that they are not simply aspirational—meaning, they are not what you think you *should be* or *could be* later in life. They are meant to represent the core of who you are all the time. That isn't to say you couldn't apply those strengths to set new goals and build the life you want to lead—but the strengths themselves are always there inside of you.

Let's dig deeper into how your five strengths already show up in your life, and where you could build upon them even more.

⊚ MY STRENGTHS EXPLORATION

Remember Sam? One of the strengths he identified was discipline. He can see that, for most of his life, he has been able to focus and do what he needed to get done in a highly disciplined way. Here's his strengths exploration for discipline:

Strength: Disciplined

This strength shows up in your (circle all that apply):

Relationships

Achievement

Personal growth

Pick a specific time this strength helped you in one of these areas. Write briefly about it here:

Being disciplined is part of how I became a good trumpet player. I had to

practice every day. That helped me get into band and also musical theater.

Now think about how this strength could help you in new ways. Identify new ways you could use this strength in your life:

1. I could use my discipline to set daily goals to get back to getting my homework done.

2. I could practice trumpet every day even if I'm not in band right now, because I love trumpet and it'll keep me good at it for the future.

◎ YOU TRY IT!

Strength: _____

This strength shows up in your (circle all that apply):

Relationships

Achievement

Personal growth

Pick a specific time this strength helped you in one of these areas. Write briefly about it here:

_____

_____

Now think about how this strength could help you in new ways. Identify two new ways you could use this strength in your life:

1. _____

_____

2. _____

_____

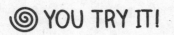 **YOU TRY IT!**

Strength: _____

This strength shows up in your (circle all that apply):

      Relationships

      Achievement

      Personal growth

Pick a specific time this strength helped you in one of these areas. Write briefly about it here:

_____

_____

Now think about how this strength could help you in new ways. Identify two new ways you could use this strength in your life:

1. _____

   _____

2. _____

   _____

Great work! Knowing what your strengths are can help you use them to build the life you want to live!

CHAPTER 14

BUILD POSITIVE SELF-TALK

What we say to ourselves is powerful. Practicing filling your own mental bucket with positive thoughts can help direct your attention to the good in you and in your life.

As we talked about in chapter 8, depression brain is a thing. Our brain likes for everything to make sense. So, when we feel a certain way, we tend to see the world in a way that lines up with our mood. When we feel sad, down, lonely, or anxious, our brain tends to see the negative in everything. This creates a negative mood/negative thinking depression spiral that keeps us feeling bad.

One way to break out of this depression spiral is to help your brain start to see the good in yourself and the world again.

"Positive thinking" can get a bad rap for being overly cheerful and not genuine. Look on the bright side! Think positively! Find the silver lining! Turn that frown upside down!

And yet, study after study finds that people who are able to think positively—who are optimistic, who handle setbacks with grace, and who speak to themselves with kindness—do better in life (Scheier and Carver 1993). They have less depression and better physical and mental health. The trick is to build positive thinking that is genuine and real.

Let's get started!

POSITIVE THINKING TIP #1: BE THE OPTIMISM YOU WANT TO SEE IN THE WORLD

Have you ever heard the saying, "The bird on the branch doesn't worry about the branch breaking, because it trusts its wings to fly"?

This is a great example of optimistic thinking. Optimism doesn't mean blindly assuming things will be good in the future. Optimism means hoping for the best but also trusting that, should things go wrong, you'll figure out a way to cope.

These are the two key parts to optimistic thinking: hope and confidence.

Hope means just that—hoping for things to go well, the way we want them to.

Confidence is the sneaky side of optimism—it is believing and trusting that, no matter how things turn out, you'll figure out a way to be okay with it.

Some optimistic thoughts:

It'll be okay.

I'll figure it out.

I can handle what comes my way.

There are many things to look forward to.

Let's Practice!

Let's imagine you have a big audition coming up for the school musical. You've been practicing a lot, but you know there are a lot of talented singers and actors at your school.

SITUATION: Big audition for the school musical.

DEPRESSION THOUGHT: I probably won't get a part. I'm probably not good enough. Maybe I shouldn't even audition.

OPTIMISTIC THOUGHT: I hope I get a good role. But even if I don't, it'll be fun to be part of the musical and I can keep practicing for the next audition.

◎ YOU TRY IT!

Think of something coming up in the near future that you're worried about or un-sure of.

SITUATION: _____

_____

DEPRESSION THOUGHT: _____

_____

OPTIMISTIC THOUGHT: _____

_____

POSITIVE THINKING TIP #2: FACING CHALLENGE WITH ENCOURAGEMENT

Life can be stressful. It can be demanding, hard, and frustrating. We can fall short at times—disappoint ourselves or others, make mistakes, or get caught unprepared.

How we think about ourselves in times of challenge can be transformative to our mood. When things are hard, if we pile on with pessimism, self-criticism, or self-blame, we will find ourselves feeling more and more depressed.

Instead, we can practice speaking to ourselves with encouragement—especially when things are stressful.

Encouragement is about giving yourself the support, confidence, and persuasion to handle challenging things.

Some encouraging thoughts:

I can do this.

I can improve.

Everyone struggles sometimes.

I have a lot of strengths to apply to this situation.

Let's Practice!

Let's imagine you didn't pass your first driving test. You've been practicing, but parallel parking is just really, really hard still. You're thinking of just canceling your next test and giving up.

SITUATION: Failed your first driving test.

DEPRESSION THOUGHT: I suck. I'm such an idiot for not being able to learn this. I'll probably never get my license.

ENCOURAGEMENT THOUGHT: Learning to drive is hard. I'm practicing and doing the best I can. Lots of people have learned how to do this and I trust I will with time.

◎ YOU TRY IT!

Think of something recently that has been hard or stressful for you.

SITUATION: _____

_____

DEPRESSION THOUGHT: _____

_____

ENCOURAGEMENT THOUGHT: _____

_____

POSITIVE THINKING TIP #3: TALK TO YOURSELF THE WAY YOU'D TALK TO OTHERS

Imagine your friend accidentally replied all to a class email with something personal meant only for the teacher. She's super embarrassed and doesn't want to go back to that class. What would you say to her?

You'd probably say things like: "It's not a huge deal. It's just a little mistake. Everybody makes them. Don't beat yourself up about it."

Now—what if *you* had sent that email? What would you have said to yourself?

Probably much less nice things. Probably you'd beat yourself up with thoughts like, "I'm such an idiot. Everyone is going to laugh at me. I'll never live this down. I'm too embarrassed to go back to school."

Learning to treat ourselves with kindness can be hard, especially if we're used to constant self-criticism and self-blame. But learning to fill our mental bucket with positive thoughts starts with our own self-talk. How we speak to ourselves matters. Let's practice building self-kindness in our thoughts and self-talk.

Let's Practice!

Imagine you wake up and immediately start thinking about all that is wrong with you and that could go wrong with the day.

SITUATION: Woke up feeling awful and incredibly negative.

DEPRESSION THOUGHT: I'm ugly. I'm boring. I'm stupid. I suck. Nothing matters.

SELF-KINDNESS THOUGHT: I am a good person. I am deserving of love. All I can do is the best I can do today.

◎ YOU TRY IT!

Think of a time recently when you found that you were thinking negative thoughts about yourself.

SITUATION: _____

_____

DEPRESSION THOUGHT: _____

_____

SELF-KINDNESS THOUGHT: _____

_____

BUILDING POSITIVE THINKING THROUGH DAILY AFFIRMATIONS

Like any new skill, practice is key to getting better. One way to build positive thinking is to have a set of personal positive affirmations that you practice daily. Great starts to daily affirmations are "I am" and "I can."

Here are some positive affirmations you might consider—but it is important to create or choose ones that are meaningful to you! Circle the ones that resonate with you most.

POSITIVE AFFIRMATIONS: WHICH RESONATE WITH YOU?

I am loved.	I am enough.	I am strong.	I am worthy.	I am capable.
I am a force.	I am bigger than my challenges.	I am grateful.	I am kind and good.	I am healthy.
I can do this.	I can handle it.	I can make this day what I want.	I can see the good in me.	I can see the good in life.
I can rise above.	I can succeed.	I can persevere.	I can thrive.	I can be happy.

IDEA! Think back to the personal strengths you identified in chapter 12. That can be a great place to find inspiration for positive affirmations.

◎ MY DAILY AFFIRMATIONS

Write down five affirmations that you can use in your day-to-day life, especially when you're feeling stuck or down. You can use the affirmations that you just circled or you can write your own!

1. _____

2. _____

3. _____

4. _____

5. _____

Now, think about *where* you'll write these affirmations and *when* you'll practice them.

Some people like to put sticky notes on their bathroom mirror. Others like to have them on a notepad next to their bed. Others like to have them written in their phone.

Where will you write your affirmations?

_____

Most teens find that reading their positive affirmations aloud in the morning helps them start their day off right. But you can also read them at bedtime, just before school, or whenever you have a hard moment.

When will you practice your affirmations?

_____

You're off to a great start filling your mental bucket with optimistic, encouraging, and self-kind thoughts!

CHAPTER 15

BUILD GRATITUDE

Gratitude is simply the behavior of being thankful. It is the ability to look around, identify, and appreciate the positives in our lives. We can be grateful for the big positives in our lives, such as having a roof over our head or good health. But we can also be grateful for the small things—from a hot cup of tea on a cold morning to the sun shining as we walk into class, expecting a quiz, only to find out the class has been canceled.

Gratitude is very powerful. Grateful people sleep better, have better relationships, and are overall happier (Sansone and Sansone 2010). And gratitude is associated with less depression.

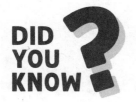

Teens who report more gratitude report more daily positive emotions and lower daily negative emotions, and can use more helpful coping strategies when stressed.

THE POWER OF GRATITUDE

How does it work? Recent research suggests that a regular gratitude practice makes us handle stress better—that gratitude makes it easier for us to access the positive thoughts and behaviors we have been learning in this workbook (Leavy et al. 2022). When we feel negative emotions, such as depression, irritability, or anxiety, our brain shuts down and only allows us to see certain thoughts and behaviors. We're likely to revert to our old, well-practiced depression responses—we get overwhelmed and then withdraw or lash out.

But when we feel positive emotions, such as gratitude, our brain opens up and we can see more options in front of us. We're able to access a wider range of thoughts and behaviors in response to life events. We can consider options beyond withdrawing or lashing out, such as reaching out for social support, solving the problem, or thinking about it in a more helpful way.

REFLECTION
REFLECTION

When you're feeling good (happy, calm, excited), do you find it is easier for you to handle stress?

Let's Get Started!

Gratitude, like any other skill we want to develop, has to be practiced on a regular basis to become a natural part of our daily lives. If we wanted to strengthen a muscle, we would work at it every day until it is strong, and then keep using it to keep it strong. Gratitude is no different!

To build our gratitude muscle, we need to practice gratitude every day. Thankfully there are many short, easy ways to build gratitude in five minutes or less every day. Here are a few fast and easy gratitude practices:

Fill Your Bucket

Find an empty jar or glass or small box and put it next to your bed along with a pad of sticky notes. Every night when you're setting your alarm or plugging your phone in to charge, take sixty seconds to write down one thing you were grateful for that day. Fold it in half and slip it into the jar. Bonus! In addition to offering a daily practice, over time your jar or box will become full with gratitude and be a great reminder.

Write It Down

You can go old-school and get a pen-and-paper journal, or go high-tech and keep a running note on your phone. However you choose to do it, each day, write down three things you're grateful for in your gratitude journal.

There's an App for That

There are many free apps that help you practice gratitude every day—and conveniently send you notifications to remember to do it! One of my favorites is Happyfeed; it's free, you can set yourself daily notifications, and it's super easy. But you can search "gratitude app" in your app store to find many other options as well.

Share the Good

Try saying "thank you" to someone in your life—a family member, friend, even the checkout person at the store—at least once a day. It'll help you notice the little things others do for you, and your ability to express your gratitude to others will strengthen those connections.

Use Your Five Senses

One thing we always have access to is our own five senses. Taking a moment every day to stop and notice what you see, hear, smell, taste, and touch can be a great way to tune in to things you can be grateful for. Perhaps it is the taste of your breakfast, the sound of the wind blowing, the colors of fall leaves, or the feeling of your sweater on your skin.

⊚ YOU TRY IT!

Use your five senses to stop and notice what is going on around you right now.

I SEE: _____

I HEAR: _____

I SMELL: _____

I TASTE: _____

I FEEL: _____

Use those things you noticed to write down three things you're grateful for right now:

I'M GRATEFUL FOR: _____

I'M GRATEFUL FOR: _____

I'M GRATEFUL FOR: _____

IDEA! Try taking it one step further—or rather, a lot of steps. Try repeating this exercise by taking a ten-minute walk, instead of simply focusing on a single moment. Once again, stop and notice what you see, hear, smell, taste, and touch, and then come up with three things you're grateful for based on what you noticed during your walk.

◎ MAKE A PLAN!

What will you do to start practicing daily gratitude? Circle the one you're most interested in, and make sure to do it or start it as soon as you get the chance.

Gratitude jar

Gratitude journal

Download an app

Say thank you

Use my five senses

When will you do this gratitude practice?

_____

How long will you do this practice for?

_____

CHAPTER 16

BUILD CONNECTION

Remember Sam from chapter 1? Sam moved to a new town and new school, and is really unhappy. He's unmotivated at school and really misses being in a music program.

Sam is also *lonely*. He misses his old friends and feels left out of their ongoing social lives. He hasn't made new friends yet. Feeling lonely is a big contributor to feeling depressed.

 A Harvard study found that the #1 predictor of happiness is social relationships. People who stay connected to others live longer, happier lives (Mineo 2017).

Have you heard of introverts and extroverts?

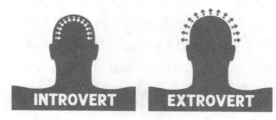

Introverts tend to:

- Prefer small groups of people

- Feel shy or overwhelmed in large social settings sometimes

- "Recharge" with alone time

Extroverts tend to:

- Love the energy of large groups

- Enjoy parties and large get-togethers

- "Recharge" with social interaction

REFLECTION *Are you more of an introvert or more of an extrovert? Is that by a lot or just a little?*

You may know whether you are more of an introvert or extrovert, but the truth is everyone is a little bit of both. Often depression gets in the way of our ability to connect with others—we withdraw, we don't want to burden others with our own mood, or we simply don't have the energy. But humans are social creatures, and some amount of social connection is good for your mental health. In this chapter you'll examine your own social style, do an inventory of your social connections, and see if there are people or relationships you'd like to lean into more.

Building social connection takes time and effort. The digital world has added a new dimension to relationship-building as well. Online connections give us more opportunity to interact with more people, but sometimes those interactions lack depth and meaning.

One of the first steps to building more social connections is to understand what kind of person you are socially. Let's get started!

WHAT'S MY SOCIAL STYLE?

One way of thinking about what kind of social person you are is whether you're more introverted or more extroverted. But recent social research has suggested that there may be more features to our social selves. This model suggests that people tend to fall into one of four social "styles" (Merrill and Reid 1981).

These styles are based on two primary qualities:

1. **TELL VERSUS ASK:** This pair of traits is about how much you feel driven to get things done and tell others what to do (high Tell) versus how much you prefer to sit back, gather information, and see what happens naturally (high Ask).

2. **PEOPLE VERSUS TASKS:** This pair of traits is about how much you attend to what you and others are feeling (high People-Focus) versus how much you prefer to focus on the task at hand, not messy human emotions (high Task-Focus).

These two qualities create four social styles:

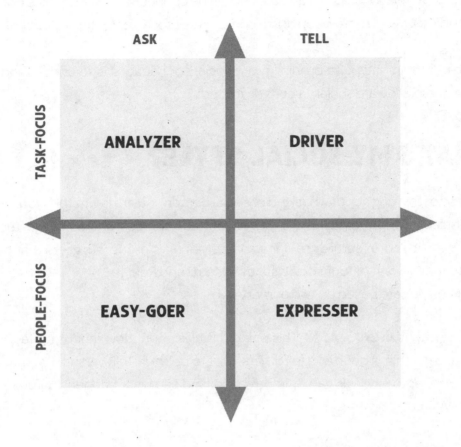

Let's learn more about each social style, and along the way you can think about whether each describes you!

The Analyzer

The analyzer is high Ask and high Task-Focus. The analyzer is often described by others as quiet, logical, and cautious in social settings. They are often very thoughtful and observant, and like to take time to form and express opinions.

The Driver

The driver is high Tell and high Task-Focus. The driver is often described by others as decisive, forceful, and determined. They often initiate social interactions and are good at getting themselves and others focused on goals they want accomplished.

The Expresser

The expresser is high Tell and high People-Focus. The expresser is often described by others as emotional, talkative, and opinionated. They often show how they feel and help others express how they feel.

The Easy-Goer

The easy-goer is high Ask and high People-Focus. The easy-goer is often described as friendly and easy to get along with. They are often good at connecting with lots of different people.

It is important to note that very few people fit perfectly into any one of these four categories. Many of us have a little of two or three or even all four inside of us, depending on the circumstances, who we're with, or even our mood.

 **REFLECTION** *Which social style or styles describe you best? Are you different in different social situations?*

WHY IS KNOWING YOUR SOCIAL STYLE HELPFUL?

We want to leverage our natural strengths to build the life we want to live. We don't want to try to fit into the box of someone else's life! Every social style above has both strengths and areas for growth—that is, areas where they can challenge themselves socially and benefit. Because of that, knowing your social style is a great way to understand what your social strengths and areas of growth are.

SOCIAL STYLES AND WHAT THEY MEAN

SOCIAL STYLE	STRENGTH	GROWTH AREA
Analyzer	Thoughtful and observant friend	Initiate social interaction Speak up
Driver	Initiate social events	Listen to others Let others lead
Expresser	Deep emotional connections	Slow down Let others speak
Easy-Goer	Easy to talk to	Initiate social interactions Offer opinions

Think about your own social strengths and areas of growth. What are you good at socially? Where could you grow?

SOCIAL INVENTORY

We need lots of different kinds of people in our lives. We need people we can trust with our deepest thoughts and feelings. We need people who will support us unconditionally. We need people who are fun to spend time with. We need people who can help us when we need something.

Below is a social inventory (Weissman et al. 2017). In the center is the person it's about—and in just a minute, that's going to be you.

First, though, let's get a better understanding of how social inventories work by looking at Sam's.

Since this is Sam's social inventory, he's in the center. Each circle around him represents people in his life in various levels of closeness.

CIRCLE 1: Very close. This may be family or friends that you trust deeply. Many people only have one or two people in this closest circle.

CIRCLE 2: Pretty close. This may be people you trust with some things or are somewhat close to.

CIRCLE 3: Not super close. This may be people you interact with but aren't super close to.

Sam's social inventory might look like this:

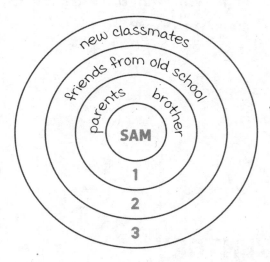

It probably would have looked different if we'd met Sam last year when he was still at his old school. He'd probably have a couple of his friends in circle 1 and more of his classmates or band friends in circle 2. But the move has really impacted his social circles.

Looking at Sam's social inventory, we might imagine that a good first social goal for him would be to try to move some new classmates, who he doesn't know well, into a closer circle.

If you were giving Sam advice, how would you suggest he start to develop closer relationships with his new classmates?

_____

_____

_____

◎ YOU TRY IT!

Now, let's figure out your social inventory. You're at the center, of course. Go ahead and fill out circles 1, 2, and 3 with the people you're close to in your own life.

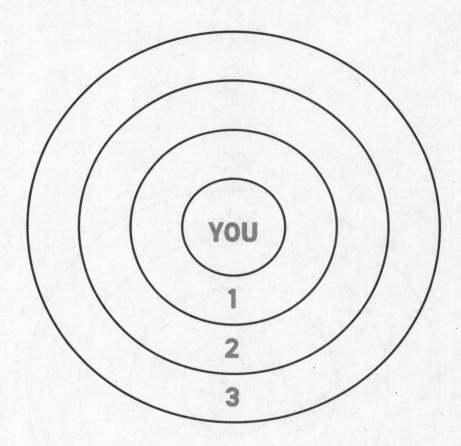

Now, let's think about your social inventory. What are some things you'd like to work on to strengthen your social circle? Are there any people in circle 2 or circle 3 that you'd like to be closer to? Are there any circles that you'd like to have more people inside of?

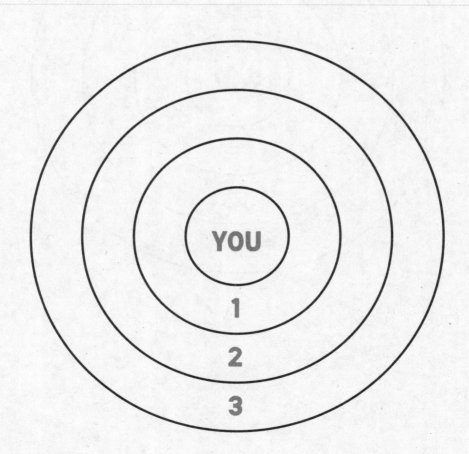

What does your social inventory tell you? Is there a circle that is pretty full already? Is there a circle that you'd like to add to?

_____

_____

_____

TIPS FOR BUILDING CONNECTION

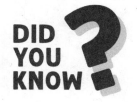

Most experts say it takes three to six months to build a new social network (Hall 2018).

Making friends and building social connection doesn't happen overnight. It takes time and effort to create meaningful relationships and fill in our social circles. Even if you haven't changed schools or towns, but are just deciding to make a change to your life—be patient. With time and persistence, you can shape the social network you want!

While sometimes it seems like some people are just better at making friends naturally, the truth is that there are some specific skills that help you connect with others.

Let's get started!

Power of Proximity

It's always easiest to connect with people you spend time with already. This may be classmates, teammates, family members, or people you do any activity with.

REFLECTION
Who do you already interact with that you'd like to be closer to?

_____

_____

Get Busy

Shared interests and hobbies are a great way to connect with others who share your passions. Getting involved in a club, sport, or online community may help you find people who share your interests.

REFLECTION
What are you involved in? Can you get more involved in that activity?

_____

_____

Speak Up

Especially if you're more Ask than Tell, it might be hard for you to initiate social interaction. But someone has to get things started! Some ideas for initiating interaction with others include:

Give a compliment

Ask a question

Ask for help

Send a text

Share a funny video

Invite a friend to do something

REFLECTION *Who in your life could you reach out to this week?*

_____

_____

Be Vulnerable

Research shows that some amount of emotional disclosure can help build closer relationships between people (Willems et al. 2020). That isn't to say you should tell a perfect stranger all your deepest, darkest secrets! But a little bit of opening up and showing your vulnerable side can sometimes invite others to do the same. This can be as simple as saying to a classmate, "This class really stresses me out," or to a sort-of-close-friend, "I'm having a hard day." You might be surprised at their positive and supportive reaction.

REFLECTION
REFLECTION *Who could you open up to a little this week? What would you tell them?*

_____

_____

◎ MAKE A PLAN!

MY SOCIAL GOAL: _____

_____

Three specific things I can do to work toward that goal:

1. _____

_____

2. _____

_____

3. _____

_____

PUTTING IT ALL TOGETHER

Depression is real. And it's not just about feeling down or sad—depression can affect every part of your life, from sleep to energy to motivation to relationships. In this workbook, you learned all of the different ways depression can affect your life. Now, let's look back on what you've learned and put it all together.

WHAT YOUR DEPRESSION LOOKS LIKE

Where do you notice your depression?

I FEEL: _____

_____

I ACT: _____

_____

I THINK: _____

_____

MY BODY: _____

_____

Depression is unique. No one person who is depressed feels or acts exactly like another person with depression. Circle all the ways that depression shows up for you:

Low motivation	Sleep too much	Can't sleep
Irritable	Cry a lot	Withdraw
Don't enjoy anything	Stressed out	Low self-esteem
Heavy body	Negative thinking	Low energy

The depression cycle keeps us stuck in a cycle of negative mood, negative thoughts, and unhelpful behaviors. Fill out the depression spiral below with a specific spiral or thought process that you've learned you experience.

Situation: _____

_____

Feeling: _____

_____

Thoughts: _____

_____

Physical symptoms: _____

_____

Behaviors: _____

_____

But there's hope! In this workbook, you learned many strategies that can take that depression spiral and turn it into an upward spiral. You learned how you can feel better, get motivated, and build the life you want to live.

The first step to combating depression is to start feeling better. And sometimes, that means going back to the basics. We worked on improving sleep and getting more physical activity to help our bodies function and build back some energy.

One way I can improve my sleep is:

_____

One way I can get more physical activity is:

_____

We also worked on handling stress better. Stress and depression often walk hand in hand, so learning to cope better when things are tough is a great way to beat depression. We worked on building a self-care toolkit so that when you're stressed, you have things that can calm you down, help you find support, and help you take care of yourself.

What are three things you can do for self-care:

1. _____

2. _____

3. _____

An important part of feeling better is recognizing when depression brain is sending us negative thoughts. We learned about the most common depression thinking traps and how to break out of them.

Which thinking trap do you fall into most often? Circle it:

Black-and-white thinking

Crystal ball

Gray-colored glasses

It's all about me

Emotion brain

The next step to battling depression is to get your life back on track. Depression messes with motivation, which can make it hard to get things done. It's easy to start falling behind on schoolwork or other goals. We worked on several strategies to help you improve motivation and focus for getting things done.

The first thing we did was work on breaking down procrastination brain. We identified the self-defeating thoughts that keep us feeling overwhelmed and worked on reframing them.

What is one of your procrastination thoughts?

_____

_____

What is a more helpful way to think about the situation?

_____

_____

Next, we learned how to break down big projects into bite-size pieces by setting SMART goals. SMART goals are goals that are specific, measurable, achievable, relevant, and time-bound.

What is one SMART goal you have for the next week?

_____

_____

Finally, we worked on strategies to build focus, such as preparing to be productive and using chunking.

What did you learn about how you can be more productive?

_____

_____

The final step to depression-proofing your life is to build up so much good that you don't have space for depression to creep back in. In the final sections of the workbook, we worked on how to build the life you want to live, by identifying your strengths, improving positive thinking, cultivating gratitude, and building connections with others.

When you're depressed, your brain is so used to thinking negative and self-critical thoughts that it can feel very unfamiliar to find more positive thoughts.

Was there a strength you identified that surprised you?

A great way to build more positive thinking is to cultivate an "attitude of gratitude." Gratitude is a very powerful emotion—it helps us experience more positive emotions and handle stress better.

What is something you are grateful for right now?

Finally, we worked on understanding the importance of building social connections and how understanding your own social style can help you do that.

What is a social goal you have for yourself?

It is important to remember that depression is a complex problem. Just like there's no one cause, there's no one solution. This workbook hopefully gave you many strategies to try—and hopefully you will find some that work for you!

Great job working through this workbook! If you want to work through any of these exercises again, you can always make blank copies of them—or in some cases, like the SMART goals, you can download extra copies of the worksheet from the free tools that go with this workbook, which you can find online.

You know the saying "Rome wasn't built in a day"? That means that it takes time to build amazing things. *You* are an amazing thing, and it will take time for you to build the life you want to live—but keep at it! Soon you'll be living the healthy, happy life you deserve.

REFERENCES

Beck, A. T. 1976. *Cognitive Therapy and the Emotional Disorders*. New York: International Universities Press.

Bradbury, N. A. 2016. "Attention Span During Lectures: 8 Seconds, 10 Minutes, or More?" *Advances in Physiology Education* 40: 509–513. https://doi.org/10.1152/advan.00109.2016.

Caplin, A., F. S. Chen, M. R. Beauchamp, and E. Puterman. 2021. "The Effects of Exercise Intensity on the Cortisol Response to a Subsequent Acute Psychosocial Stressor." *Psychoneuroendocrinology* 131: 105336. https://doi.org/10.1016/j.psyneuen.2021.105336.

Daly, M. 2022. "Prevalence of Depression Among Adolescents in the U.S. From 2009 to 2019: Analysis of Trends by Sex, Race/Ethnicity, and Income." *Journal of Adolescent Health* 70(3): 496–499. https://doi.org/10.1016/j.jadohealth.2021.08.026.

Doran, G. T. 1981. "There's a S.M.A.R.T. Way to Write Management's Goals and Objectives." *Management Review* 70: 35–36.

Duan, W. 2016. "The Benefits of Personal Strengths in Mental Health of Stressed Students: A Longitudinal Investigation." *Quality of Life Research* 25: 2879–2888. https://doi.org/10.1007/S11136-016-1320-8.

Dunn E. C., R. C. Brown, Y. Dai, J. Rosand, N. R. Nugent, A. B. Amstadter, J. W. Smoller. 2015. "Genetic Determinants of Depression: Recent Findings and Future Directions." *Harvard Review of Psychiatry* 23: 1–18. https://doi.org/10.1097/HRP.0000000000000054.

Hall, J. A. 2018. "How Many Hours Does It Take to Make a Friend?" *Journal of Social and Personal Relationships* 36: 1278–1296. https://doi.org/10.1177/0265407518761225.

Kessler, R. C., P. Berglund, O. Demler, R. Jin, K. R. Merikangas, and E. E. Walters. 2005. "Lifetime Prevalence and Age-of-Onset Distributions of DSM-IV Disorders in the National Comorbidity Survey Replication." *Archives of General Psychiatry* 62: 593–602. https://doi.org/10.1001/archpsyc.62.6.593.

Kroenke, K., R. L. Spitzer, and J. B. W. Williams. 1999. Patient Health Questionnaire-9 (PHQ-9) [Database record]. APA PsycTests. https://doi.org/10.1037/t06165-000.

Leavy, B., B. H. O'Connell, and D. O'Shea. 2022. "Gratitude, Affect Balance, and Stress Buffering: A Growth Curve Examination of Cardiovascular Responses to a Laboratory Stress Task." *International Journal of Psychophysiology* 183: 103–116. https://doi.org/10.1016/j.ijpsycho.2022.11.013.

Merrill, D. W., and R. H. Reid. 1981. *Personal Styles and Effective Performance.* New York: CRC Press.

Mineo, L. 2017. "Good Genes Are Nice, but Joy Is Better." *The Harvard Gazette,* April 11. https://news.harvard.edu/gazette/story/2017/04/over-nearly-80-years-harvard-study-has-been-showing-how-to-live-a-healthy-and-happy-life.

Monroe, S. M., and K. L. Harkness. 2005. "Life Stress, the 'Kindling' Hypothesis, and the Recurrence of Depression: Considerations from a Life Stress Perspective." *Psychological Review* 112: 417–445. https://doi.org/10.1037/0033-295X.112.2.417.

National Institutes of Health. 2020. "Tired or Wired: Caffeine and Your Brain." *NIH New in Health,* October. https://newsinhealth.nih.gov/2020/10/tired-or-wired.

Park, N., and C. Peterson. 2006. "Moral Competence and Character Strengths Among Adolescents: The Development and Validation of the Values in Action Inventory of Strengths for Youth." *Journal of Adolescence* 29: 891–909.

Paruthi S., L. J. Brooks, C. D'Ambrosio, W. A. Hall, S. Kotagal, R. M. Lloyd, et al. 2016. "Recommended Amount of Sleep for Pediatric Populations: A Consensus Statement of the American Academy of Sleep Medicine." *Journal of Clinical Sleep Medicine* 12: 785–786. https://doi.org/10.5664/jcsm.5866.

Paulch, A. E., S. Bajpai, D. R. Bassett, M. R. Carnethon, U. Ekelund, K. R. Evenson, et al. 2022. "Daily Steps and All-Cause Mortality: A Meta-Analysis of 15 International Cohorts." *The Lancet Public Health* 7: E219–E228. https://doi.org/10.1016/S2468 -2667(21)00302-9.

Sansone, R. A., and L. A. Sansone. 2010. "Gratitude and Well Being: The Benefits of Appreciation." *Psychiatry* 7: 18–21.

Scheier, M. F., and C. S. Carver. 1993. "On the Power of Positive Thinking: The Benefits of Being Optimistic." *Current Directions in Psychological Science* 2: 26–30. https://doi .org/10.1111/1467-8721.ep10770572.

Seligman, M. E. P., and M. Csikszentmihalyi. 2000. "Positive Psychology: An Introduction." *American Psychologist* 55: 5–14. https://doi.org/10.1037/0003-066X.55.1.5.

Suni, E. 2023. "Sleep Drive and Your Body Clock." SleepFoundation.org. https://www .sleepfoundation.org/circadian-rhythm/sleep-drive-and-your-body-clock.

Tobin, D. L., K. A. Holroyd, R. V. Reynolds, and J. K. Wigal. 1989. "The Hierarchical Factor Structure of the Coping Strategies Inventory." *Cognitive Therapy and Research* 13: 343–361. https://doi.org/10.1007/BF01173478.

Weissman, M. M., J. C. Markowitz, and G. L. Klerman. 2017. *The Guide to Interpersonal Psychotherapy*, updated and expanded ed. Oxford, UK: Oxford University Press.

Willems, Y. E., C. Finkenauer, and P. Kerkhof. 2020. "The Role of Disclosure in Relationships." *Current Opinion in Psychology* 31: 33–37. https://doi.org/10.1016/j.co psyc.2019.07.032.

More ⏱ Instant Help Books for Teens

An Imprint of New Harbinger Publications

DON'T LET YOUR EMOTIONS RUN YOUR LIFE FOR TEENS, SECOND EDITION

Dialectical Behavior Therapy Skills for Helping You Manage Mood Swings, Control Angry Outbursts, and Get Along with Others

978-1684037360 / US $18.95

THE ANXIETY AND DEPRESSION WORKBOOK FOR TEENS

Simple CBT Skills to Help You Deal with Anxiety, Worry, and Sadness

978-1684039197 / US $22.95

OVERCOMING SUICIDAL THOUGHTS FOR TEENS

CBT Activities to Reduce Pain, Increase Hope, and Build Meaningful Connections

978-1684039975 / US $18.95

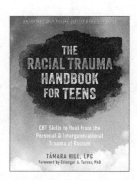

THE RACIAL TRAUMA HANDBOOK FOR TEENS

CBT Skills to Heal from the Personal and Intergenerational Trauma of Racism

978-1648480126 / US $17.95

THE TEEN GIRL'S SURVIVAL JOURNAL

Your Space to Learn, Reflect, Explore, and Take Charge of Your Mental Health

978-1648482861 / US $18.95

PUT YOUR WORRIES HERE

A Creative Journal for Teens with Anxiety

978-1684032143 / US $18.95

🌱 **new harbinger** publications

· 1-800-748-6273 / newharbinger.com

(VISA, MC, AMEX / prices subject to change without notice)

Follow Us 📷 ❏ 𝕏 ▶ 𝔭 in ♪ ⑥

Don't miss out on new books from New Harbinger.
Subscribe to our email list at **newharbinger.com/subscribe** 🖱

Amy Mezulis, PhD, is a clinical psychologist specializing in adolescent mental health. She is cofounder and chief clinical officer of Joon Care, a teletherapy practice for teens and young adults. Her research has been sponsored by the National Institute of Mental Health (NIMH) and the American Psychology Association (APA), and she has authored or coauthored articles for dozens of publications, including *Cognitive Therapy and Research*, *Journal of Cognitive Psychotherapy*, and *Harvard Review of Psychiatry*.

Foreword writer **Janet Shibley Hyde, PhD**, is professor emerit of psychology and gender and women's studies at the University of Wisconsin—Madison. She is the recipient of the James McKeen Cattell Award from the Association for Psychological Science, for distinguished achievements in psychological science.

Did you know there are **free tools** you can download for this book?

Free tools are things like **worksheets**, **guided meditation exercises**, and **more** that will help you get the most out of your book.

You can download free tools for this book— whether you bought or borrowed it, in any format, from any source—from the New Harbinger website. All you need is a NewHarbinger.com account. Just use the URL provided in this book to view the free tools that are available for it. Then, click on the "download" button for the free tool you want, and follow the prompts that appear to log in to your NewHarbinger.com account and download the material.

You can also save the free tools for this book to your **Free Tools Library** so you can access them again anytime, just by logging in to your account! Just look for this button on the book's free tools page.

+ Save this to my free tools library

If you need help accessing or downloading free tools, visit **newharbinger.com/faq** or contact us at **customerservice@newharbinger.com**.